CAPTAIN RANDOM AND THE STRATOS CONUNDRUM

Captain Random and the Stratos Conundrum

Hayden Gribble

Book FOUR in the CAPTAIN RANDOM saga

For all the stars in
our galaxies

CONTENTS

AUTHOR'S NOTE

The events of this book take place directly after CAPTAIN RANDOM AND THE RAINBOW CHASERS, so be sure to read that exciting tale before this one!

1

AFTERMATH

Unearthly sounds filled the decimated hangar. A wind raged through the vast metal walls, and the small fires that had erupted, scattered like tiny beacons of destruction, whirled their orange flames in unison as the strong breeze blew through them.

The debris of the gantry that had once been held firmly suspended forty feet above the ground began to fall. Screams from stranded beings, terrified and trapped in their surroundings, cowered with arms held high, protecting their heads as the heavy metal smashed on top of them. The screams died and were replaced by the clatter and contact of metal on metal. Explosions began to ripple and tear holes in the walls and floor.

It had become a hall of devastation.

A silver ship, about a hundred feet in height and situated right in the middle of the hangar was fading out of existence as the noise of the wind grew stronger.

Further screams of despair rang out as a few of the survivors had clambered over the falling rubble towards the magic ship but it was too late.

They were confined to their death.
Balls of fire burst the seams of the floorboards and the survivors began to scatter. Its sporadic nature suggested a series of bombs but to those trapped they would have considered that impossible for a ship that had such tight security.

None of this was in the minds of the terrified people who were still aboard. It was now a fight to get off the ship before it was too late. Escape pods were the only option left to them before the once grand ship fell out of the sky and disintegrated in the Earth's atmosphere.

In all the ruins, the strewn mounds of rubble, lay the aggressor. A man, corrupt by power, believing his own god complex, who promised those in his employ that the invasion would be successful, that they were doing the right thing, lay broken.

Immobile yet still alive, he began to open his eyes.
Groaning in agony, a thought kept ringing in his head.

How had it all gone so wrong?
The heat of the flames licked against the side of the man's face as he lay facing the ceiling in a room of de-

struction and death. All the prostrate man could feel around him was the violent waves of doom as he came to.

Shaking his head, the man groaned like somebody who had been beaten against a brick wall for over an hour. He didn't know how long he had been unconscious and in a way he didn't care.

He had failed.
And now the fallen was stirring and knew that he was finished.

The sound of the ruined metal timber falling towards him made his skin go cold. With his eyes blinking open and shut, he struggled to free himself from his temporary prison.

Staring into the burning abyss of his once oh so magnificent ship, he was pinned by the falling debris to the floor.

Although aware of his perilous position, he struggled to remember what had precisely happened.

He remembered his plan. Oh, how he had worked on it.

He had spent years plotting the attack and after using the millions of Stellerpounds he had at his disposal – not so much earned but stolen through his many business schemes, and the money he had conned out of fellow competitors in the financial market, he was able to do what nobody from his home planet of Draxo had done in over four centuries – reclaim the Earth.

Draxo was one of the first Earth colonies to settle out of the solar system. It was uninhabited and after years of research it was chosen for colonisation to help move the population of the Earth – which was stretching to overcrowding in the big urban areas – to all corners of the galaxy.

And so, with the numbers in the population at breaking point, great ships, built to hold thousands of humans in suspended sleep set off on their long jour-ney, with a crew who took it in turns to pilot them within these suspension cycles and made sure the passengers got to their new world safely.

Many were jealous at those who had been selected for the voyage to Draxo. It was a beautiful planet, rich with emerald green skies and mauve fields. The first human inhabitants were not used to this strange colour scheme but they grew to love it.

It was like no other planet in its system and as far as they knew it had never been inhabited before.

However, it wasn't long until their new paradise succumbed to the same problems that the colonists had experienced on Earth.

The colonists were placed in suspended animation for the decade long journey, as was an abundant supply of food and water, not to mention a self-servicing plantation chamber that would enable crops and vegetation to flourish while they slept.

It was to be a new golden age.

Upon landing, the scientists who had joined the colonists on the journey had taken samples of the soil and rainfall as soon as they awoke from their slumber.

The probes they had sent from Earth had been accurate, the soil was able to sustain the crops and the atmosphere was not poisonous. If anything, it was healthier than the over populated and polluted mother planet.

There was a high bombardment of positive neutrons in the air and the new settlers were in a better frame of mind once there.

The planet was tranquil, peaceful and the need for work was more of a hobby as greed was not a common trait.

Unfortunately, Draxo did also have its drawbacks.

There was a nutrient in the soil that meant it was rancid after a week.

They could combat this by managing the supplies appropriately, but as generations came and went and the surplus population grew, famine came and took the lives of some of the colonists. The designated leaders, whose predecessors had been designated on the first voyage and whose roles were inherited, pleaded for aid from the mother planet but it never came. Draxo, for reasons they did not understand, had been cut off and left alone.

And so the planet lay dying, weak and helpless, until the ruler Draxo, an ambitious and some would say reckless King, decided that they should make the Earth pay for what they had done.

Ordering repairs to be made to the ship that had carried them to Draxo centuries earlier, and enlisting the help of those who had come to the planet over the years of his rule, the plans for war began.

The money he had acquired and stolen, along with the technology that was culled from other races during his reign, made him strong and determined to bring the Earth to its knees.

Many of his subjects disagreed with his vision of war and violence.

Some were convinced that the power had gone to his head and as punishment, the King outlawed many and accused them of treason.

The once happy, peaceful humans of Draxo were now ruled with an iron fist and forced into a war with their own people.

The King gave himself a name that struck fear into his subjects and those who were loyal to him. Together they equated to an army that ensured that the King's life was kept safe from the rebels who tried to kill him before Draxo was beyond redemption.

That name was Stratos.

Stratos abandoned Draxo, leaving behind the weak, feeble and those who opposed him, to die. Ordering his troops aboard the ship that brought them to what had been their Eden, Stratos and his army placed themselves in suspended animation and set the coordinates to auto-pilot back to Earth.

The Army was a strong force of twenty thousand, with advanced weaponry that had been stolen from the aliens whom visited Draxo and lived to regret it, and now they were more than a match for the planet.

Whatever the conditions and no matter how surprised the peoples of the Earth would be, a ship that was once built to bring peace and new beginnings was now an armoured battle craft set on a course to destroy those who had stranded them.

The plans that had been made were meticulous to the last detail.

A sensor was set to alarm the forces if they were under attack or if an obstacle dangerous enough to cause danger to the mission meant that evasive action would be needed. At that point, they would simply wake up and destroy it.

For the first few years however they were mostly undisturbed, safe in momentary sleep, waiting for the moment they had been preparing for.

It soon became clear though, that even though communication had been lost decades earlier, Earth knew that they were coming.

As soon as the ship, now called the Commodore after the engineer that originally made her, scraped the fringes of the Solar System, a fleet of galactic fighters, small and slick in design like an ancient World War II spitfire plane, hung in the sky like a spiders web, waiting for the unwitting fly to fall into the trap.

Fifty in number, the fleet were ready, and that meant the peoples of the Earth were too.

When Stratos awoke to the sound of gun fire on his vessel, he was taken aback by the trap, but in no way unprepared.

Back on Draxo, he heard rumours that the rebels had got word to those lucky aliens who had escaped the bleak prisoners of war camps that stained the planet like blood on a flower.

The word must have got out about what he was planning. Earth knows what we are going to do, he thought to himself, but they will be no match for us.

Ships fell hard like hailstones as the Commodore showed the fleet the full might of its destructive power. The battle raged for two hours. Although slightly damaged, the shields that had been stolen by more advanced races kept most of the fire at bay.

The firepower at Stratos' disposal was devastating. One by one the little fighters were destroyed, the pilots inside trapped in the burning craft and fated to a fiery end.

Then the moment of retreat came when the ships were forced to flee, their mission failed. Licking their wounds, the armies of Earth were defeated. With minimal casualties and a regained sense of willpower and determination, Stratos had won.

Now they had penetrated the Solar System, the Commodore continued its journey of death. Following their excursion past Pluto, the armies of the solar system banded together, in a way that they hadn't done in centuries.

All the political disagreements and differences in opinion that separated the planet were forgotten for the time being.

The only planet that decided not to help the Earth was Mars, whose lifeforms elected to remain hidden from their neighbours, knowing full well what destruction the human race would bring to the red planet if they were detected and known about by the wider population. An outbreak of a contagious disease had also confined them below ground for centuries.

Living in fear and trapped on a diseased world, they watched as the ships from Earth and Mercury took off to hold the Warship away, knowing the effort was in vain.

No matter how big in number the defensive parties were, or potentially successful the campaigns were, nothing could stop the gigantic offense from lumber-ing on through the System. Now only a matter of weeks away from their final destination, Stratos relished the fight he faced.

He kept his best soldiers awake, depriving them of the sweet comfort of sleep and ordered that they stay at their posts, taking it in turns to look out and attack.

One by one the command posts that led to the world of mankind were ceased, purged and eradicated. Slaves were taken, many were slaughtered and it fed Stratos' lust for revenge.

It was as though he absorbed the attacks and let them fester in his mind, further polluting his thoughts and filling his imagination with perverse images of destruction and power. The Commodore was like a cancer wiping through the stars and obliterating all in its path. It seemed as though nothing could stop it.

Until one day, the day that Stratos let his guard down.

Repairs were required as the Commodore began to feel the brunt of the storms of battle it had faced. Shield capacity was strong, but not as strong as it could have been. The loyal followers of the man who would be King, fearful of their own lives, worked endlessly to repair the ship. Some even succumbed to their weakness and kept awake, whilst some starved to the point of death and began to slip away.

Stratos was as relentless and unfeeling as stone through a plain glass window. He killed those who were too weak to fight or work, knowing that there were still many in suspended animation he could call on.

Work conditions were appalling and his armies were making mistakes thanks to it.

Following a devastating fight on the rings of Jupiter, the Commodore was badly damaged. It was the first time since the ship had started its invasion that it had been defeated. Loathing the decision he had to make, Stratos ordered his subjects to retreat and they fled.

It was just at this moment, unbeknownst to him, that a mysterious ship seemingly materialised out of nowhere on board. Out stepped a purple skinned, spiky haired male, who held himself high and strode into this world of hate like he owned the stage, accom-panied by his three friends.

A tall, strong looking female with her black coloured hair dangling in a thick plait, a kind and yet dangerous robot who was in the shape of a skateboard and a young blonde haired scruffy male who looked roughly the same age as the woman with dark hair. The purple one carried an unearthly feel and a yearning to wreak havoc about him. They were wanderers, rebels, chaos bringers.

It was as if they had not been home in a very, very long time.

They brought with them a sense of experience be-yond the stars and soon they went about destroying Stratos' world from the inside, like a virus in a computer mainframe.

Stratos, lying in the rubble, winced as he tried to move.

He opened his dry, blood stained lips and uttered the only thing that was in his mind.

'Random,' he spluttered as he struggled to move, dry spit barking from lungs.

'RANDOM!'

Another explosion gave birth to a glow of fire that growled at Stratos like an animal. Every sinew of his being was broken, beaten. His body told him to stay where he was, accept his fate and embrace the inevitable.

His mind spoke another language to him, one of survival, vengeance and hate. The pain worsened now his eyes were open. The ambition, like the fire now raging throughout the Commodore, burned brightly.

He had to get out - and nothing was going to stop him.

At first his small movements ached, and then the pain really set in. Hot, searing pain that shot through his veins and boiled within every sinew in his body. Stratos knew it was futile to try and guess how and where the breaks had occurred. It felt as though nearly every bone in his body was broken.

By all rights, he should already be dead; he knew that, especially after falling seventy feet from a disintegrating gantry onto the stone cold floor below.

From every angle, the man who called himself Random had beaten him.

How an intruder like him aligned himself with rebels who were hiding in the store rooms and saved both himself and his allies and left the others to die was incredible. To have compassion and show no remorse in equal measure was a personality trait that puzzled Stratos and led him to believe that this man was not like any other he had encountered.

To him, Random's behaviour was like that of an old campaigner, whose eyes only reveal his true intentions and his full ruthlessness to his enemies and hides them from those who trust him.

Every inch began to feel like a mile but Stratos was undeterred. Crawling away from the rubble and watching the panic unfold around him, the pain he felt illuminated from his blood shot eyes and pathed the way out of danger.

Desperately, Stratos searched the room, which glowed a brilliant orange. The screams of his men, supposedly the best of the best, the ones he personally picked and oversaw the training of, ran around like headless chickens.

The feeling of depression and imminent doom hung like a fog amongst the smoke.

The Commodore was breaking up around him, his beloved ship, the one that was meant to bring to

Stratos his dream of revenge, was going down faster than the Titanic in Earth stories of old.

The ship slipped even further out of space towards the planet it was supposed to conquer, pulling away at its metallic seams in the atmosphere.

Many will have already perished, sucked into the vacuum of space or fated to a fiery grave but Stratos was not thinking about them at all. Although he was the King, he wasn't going to go down with the ship.

Still crawling, Stratos' eyes were firmly on the prize. His salvation and only means of escape lay mere metres away.

Through the fire and smoke and his own blurred vision, he spotted an escape pod on the opposite side of the hanger to where he had laid.

In all the confusion, and although some had escaped and were bound to be picked up by the Space Seals, only one remained empty. Its red, vacant light lit the way.

He was nearly there.

The pain was put to the back of his mind for the time being, he could worry about it later.

Safety was so close for him now. VWOOOSSSHHH!

An explosion, so ferocious in its manner, rocked the hangar.

Stratos stopped his hellish trek and lay prostrate on the floor.

Looking up, he started to feel his broken body being dragged back towards the rubble pit he had awoken in.

Struggling to fit his fingers in a metal grill on the floor, Stratos blinked into the void behind him. The hanger was silent now. No more screams or desperate struggles to get off the doomed craft.

Stratos was now alone in the hanger; the only company he had now was the vast hole that had replaced the hull.

He watched as his faithful soldiers, the ones who had shared his dreams and those who he despised were floating lifelessly in the black, unforgiving silence of space.

A wind that sent a chill along his spine was still tempting the fallen leader to a silent death.

Holding on with the last remaining effort of his being, Stratos, who knew that the only strength he had left in his body was now in his arms, edged his way along the grill the last few feet to the escape pod door.

Grimacing and screaming until his lungs began to burn, Stratos reached out for the release button. His fingertips reached out like a child seeking the attention of its mother.

Just a little further.

More fire and sparks licked his face with vicious intent and the icy touch of deep space dragging him towards death.

His screams inaudible over the vacuum

that wanted to embrace him, Stratos' last ounce of strength hurled him onto the button.

In a split second the escape pod door, which was about six feet in height, whipped open. Feeling along the wall inside the pod, Stratos found a hold and swung himself inside, snapping the door shut.

He had made it.

Now, the fun really started.

Sliding to the floor once more, Stratos panted as he rocked about in the little pod. The turbulence created an unstable yet safe environment for the Warlord to tend to his wounds.

He knew, however, that to elude his enemies from Earth and escaping too early, he would have to release the pod at just the right moment.

He felt that it was coming soon.

Around the pod, more and more chunks of the Commodore collapsed, splitting through the stress of the fractures that had been created by the internal damage of the explosions.

The hole that had been torn in the hull was now replicating all over the ancient ship. The loss of life was insurmountable and disturbing.

Not all of the rebels had been lucky enough to escape, something Random had promised they would succeed in doing.

The majority of them were among the first to be picked up by the salvage ship, warning that those who

followed were Stratos' personal army, fleeing like flies
from a carcass.

The rebels watched from a safe distance as the
Commodore, a ship that set sail on a mission of peace and
prosperity that had become one of war and death, in a blaze
of fury, perished for good.

Stratos flicked the jettison switch as soon as he felt the
force of the first shock wave. The sound was like that of
an atom bomb and it deafened the lone survivor. He had
found no time to secure himself in one of the grey seats
that sat to the side of the pod. The pod was roughly the
size of a cupboard and would have only fitted two people
but with the extra room available, Stratos' tormented
frame was thrown to the far side of the pod, screaming as
the gravity created by the shock waves crushed him.
Before long, Stratos closed his eyes, giving in to the bliss
of unconsciousness. His body was broken and he now had
no feeling below his waist. Only willpower had brought
him out of his destiny of fire.

He had cheated death. It was up to the pod now to
carry his nearly lifeless form to safety.

Whilst his eyes were closed, a mirage of thoughts
flowed through his mind. There was no point answering
the questions he had now, he should just let them go, give
in to the embrace of sleep and worry about it later.

The pod tore away along with the rest of the debris that once formed the magnificent form of the Commodore. Since its rockets were no longer firing, it could be easily mistaken as a spare part, a piece of a puzzle that was torn away from its body and now littered the black, empty space above Earth. The final explosion had been impressive with the look of a huge firework.

Earth was safe yet again, thanks to the strange purple man and his friends.

The alien with the mysterious silver ship had come and gone and brought with him a world of destruction. His name had betrayed his actions. He wasn't a saviour; he was a bringer of death.

Debris began to shower the Earth, falling over the isolating desolation of Antarctica. Only a few colonies were brave enough to set up home on such an un-inhabitable plain. It was here that the pod carrying Stratos was slowly heading for. The rest of the debris would break up in the atmosphere.

The capsule however, temporarily home to one of the worst War criminals in the history of the universe, was on its final journey.

Only the course Stratos thought he was taking, he would never actually complete. Something strange was happening outside in the mists of space, something that would alter the course of the universe. An anomaly was about to occur and Stratos wasn't actually heading towards the planet he once had desires upon conquering. No, he was to arrive in a place far stranger than the third rock from the sun.

With no more shock waves to hold him against the wall, Stratos' unconscious body crumpled on the floor. It fell like a rag doll and it was hard to believe that this bloody, sickening mess was once that of a strong, evil megalomaniac. His ego would never allow anybody to see him in this weakened, defeated shape.

He was alone, wounded almost beyond recognition but he was not finished. No matter how badly injured he was, he would rebuild, grow stronger than he was before and live to serve his one purpose, his only calling in life.

To kill Random.

2

A QUIET PLACE

Far away in a distant solar system, the light of a thousand stars and suns reflected off the sleek, metallic hull of the ship known as the Venus II.

As it sailed majestically through the blackness of space, it lit up like a beacon of style and sophistication. It was truly one of the most appealing space ships this side of Orion's Belt. But inside, the crew of the Venus II were feeling far from regal. In fact, after their latest ordeal, they were highly willing to never bump into another King or Queen or ruler of any kind ever again!

Jake sat on the side of his bed, running a towel through his shaggy blonde hair with all the tenderness and care of a butcher with a new-born calf. He was so rough, it was as though he didn't want any of it there in the first place. He hadn't washed it, it was something he had started doing to release his fury and felt healthier than punching a wall.

'Exiled!' he muttered loud enough for the person in the bedroom opposite his own to hear. 'I ask you!'

Anji hadn't asked. In fact, she had been very quiet. Ever since Spectronia. Ever since the Zedron Flux.

Ever since Random had collapsed and changed colour.

They had bundled their unconscious friend back on board the ship but before they left, with their heads hanging shamefully for what he had done, Random's normally vibrant purple skin complexion, unique to his planet of Rodas, had changed. Now, his pigmentation was split down the middle. His left hand side was as blue as sapphires swimming in a sunlit ocean. On his right, crimson blood red like the aftermath of a battlefield.

Their robotic friend, fondly named Skateboard for his resemblance to a little board with four wheels some people in the universe like to ride upon. As soon as the ship was up in the big black, he had shared his feelings with his companions.

'I've been concerned for some time,' he had said to them.

'Well then, why didn't you tell us?' said Anji, her tone bordering on anger.

'Miss, I was not at liberty to disclose such information. I was keeping an eye on the situation, seeing if it improved. Random and I have been discussing the matter and until now I didn't have the slightest inclination to break his confidentiality. The Captain has a right to his privacy.'

'Nice to know that he didn't feel like he could talk to us!' scoffed Jake.

'Actually, when we were trapped in the cave earlier, he started telling me something. I could tell that he was struggling. He seemed to have more on his mind than he was letting on,' Anji said awkwardly.

Jake looked indignantly at his two friends.
'Oh, right, well I see I'm not included in this heart-to-heart club!'

'Don't be so childish, Jake,' snapped Anji. 'Our friend could be in terrible danger.'

Jake sighed.
'I'm sorry Anj, Skateboard. I just...well, if you'll allow me back in the club, I'm a little scared.'

'Me too,' Anji smiled, putting a reassuring arm around her friend.

'We all are, Sir,' said Skateboard. He left the mid-section and retreated down a corridor, past the living quarters and into the medi-bay. The sound of his wheels clanked against the metal floor as he whirred into the doorway. The medi-bay was a brilliant wash of sterile white, with two beds lying side-by-side. It was the first time in quite a while that anyone had occupied those beds and for the second time it was the same patient who lay still within the silk sheets.

Skateboard thrust himself onto his hind wheels and his body rose up to get a better look at the occupant.

Anji and Jake followed in after him and joined Skateboard at Random's bedside.

The Rodasian was flat on his back, still, no sign of life. He had a tube sticking out of his mouth that was linked to a futuristic bank of machinery.

His skin was wet and clammy and apart from the slightest twinge of activity in the corners of his eyes, there was no sign that he would be getting up anytime soon.

Anji's mind flittered back to the vision of Random on that cliff top, the Zedron Flux held aloft in his hands, using it as a threat to repel an invasion force of what resembled Egyptian gods called the Osirons who in their pyramid ships had desires to hold the Flux in their grasp and rule the entire universe.

That's how powerful the Zedron Flux was. Whoever attained it was gifted sheer omnipotent power, enough to bring life or death to the farthest corners of the cosmos.

And there he had stood, Random, with the power of the gods.

Then just when all hope was lost, as a weapon of supreme power was about to split the entire planet of

Spectronia and wipe out the peaceful race of Spectronians, Random was forced to do the unthinkable.

He had opened the Flux and absorbed its power.

From their vantage point far away, Anji, Jake and Skateboard had watched in horror as their friend was consumed by its godly green glow and as he levitated, the force of the Flux burning like fire through his body, he used its awesome might against the Osirons and one-by-one, their invasion fleet fizzled out of existence.

He had saved a planet, a whole race of life, but in doing so had wiped out another.

Random had committed genocide to try to avert genocide.

As the Flux returned to its safe compartment and was relinquished to a man who had risked everything to get it to safety, Random had slumped to the ground.

And now here they were, unaware of the effects such an devastating incident could have had on his body.

Whatever it had done, the Flux had had a devastating effect on the boy.

He lay there, still and silent. Apart from a smudge of dirt on his face, there was no sign that Random had seen any physical injury. But as the most impossible person Anji and Jake had ever met lay motionless, the situation was worrying for them all.

'This is terrible,' Jake stated the obvious.

'What are his life signs saying Skateboard?' Anji squinted at the virtual readouts on the monitor on the wall above his head.

'He is stable, for now, that's what we need to worry about, but we must get him somewhere where he can be treated properly.'

'Treated for what?' asked Jake. 'Do you think the Flux did this to him?'

'It's highly possible.'

'We've seen him do some highly impossible things before, but that Flux was something else,' said Anji. She parked herself on the spare bed. 'I saw it. Close up. And I could understand why Lon wanted it so bad. All of that energy. All of that power.'

'It ran right through him, polluted every cell in his body. We can only imagine the damage it might have caused,' said Skateboard.

'So you're saying that he might never recover?' Jake's eyes looked panicked.

'I'm not a doctor, sir, so I don't want to panic either of you. The best thing we can do now is to try and find somewhere that can help him.'

His circuits whirred loudly.

'Goodness me! Just look at you two!'

Anji and Jake glanced down at their clothes. They were torn and smeared with the rainbow coloured dirt of Spectronia.

'Get out of here at once! This is a sterile unit, now out, out, out!'

He shooed them out of the room, with little protest from either of them. As soon as they were clear the medi-bay door slid shut behind them.

'He's right,' said Anji. 'We'd better take a shower.'

'Together?!' asked Jake with a mixture of hope and curiosity.

Skateboard heard the slap from inside the medi-bay and tutted before producing a small vacuum cleaner from a utility cupboard and proceeded to tidy up their mess.

*

Anji stepped from the shower feeling like a new person. She covered herself with a towel dressing down and spun her thick wet hair into another before flinging it back over her shoulders.

Sliding into her slippers, she joined Jake in his room. 'So that's the real reason why you are feeling sore, because you never got to say goodbye to, what was her name? Bow?'

'Row,' Jake corrected, chucking his towel to the floor and flopping his head into his hands, his cheeks resting on his palms making him look like a furry apple on two plates.

'Don't worry, I'm sure there will be plenty of other exotic, beautiful women out there in this wide old cosmos to not be attracted to you.'

Jake looked at his friend and let out a short laugh. 'Just because you haven't met Prince Charming yet.' 'Jake I'm 13!' she laughed. 'I'm not old enough to have met anyone yet, let alone Prince Charming. Anyway, don't you think we have more important things to think about right now?'

He nodded.

'Yeah, I suppose you're right.'

'We girls normally are,' she smiled. Jake saw that naughty twinkle in her eye.

'God, I'm so glad that it's you I ran away from the Earth with. For someone who is on a spaceship a zillion miles away from home, you know how to keep me grounded!'

'I do my best...I just wish there was something I could do to help Random.'

'Anj, what did he say to you, in that cave?'
'Nothing. He was acting peculiarly. When he was unconscious, it was like he was fighting someone invis-ible.'

'Oh great, that's all we need. First the Sandman, now the invisible man!'

'It might have been a bad dream, for all I could see, but he was...off...the whole time we were together on that planet. Something was not quite right.'

'It definitely isn't now,' scoffed Jake. 'Look, he'll be alright. He will get better. I'm sure of it.'

'Let's hope so,' said Anji, her head rested on Jake's shoulder. 'Why red and blue?'

'Didn't he say that was the colour of his people?'

'Yes, but I didn't think he meant that they were both of them. What if the Flux has done something to his DNA?'

'Okay Doctor Gummadi, like what?'

'I don't know, just…' she gave up. 'Anyway, I'd better get dressed. I'll see you in a bit.'

'Okay,' said Jake as he picked the towel up and started to ruffle his hair like he was using sandpaper on a piece of wood.

'You want to be careful you don't go bald doing it like that,' Anji chuckled as she left the room.

Jake paused and then laughed nervously to himself. He opened the towel and stared at the strands of hair that lay entangled in the soft wool. Slowly, he returned the towel to his head and patted his hair softly.

*

He lay in the dirt barely able to breathe. The liberty of air was indescribably painful. But he didn't want the pain to end. He wanted to harness it. Keep him alive. Maintain his mission objective.

The sun glared down through the broken ruins of the pod. It poured into Stratos' little world like volcanic fire. He tried not to look up directly into it, but when he looked down he wished he hadn't.

There was a hydraulic pipe where his thigh should have been. He ground his teeth as he realised that the pain in his leg was now greater than the pain in his back. Or what was left of his leg.

He snarled like a rabid dog, foaming at the mouth, trying to grit the spaces where his teeth used to be. A horrible throbbing sensation emitted from his fresh new wound. He was losing a lot of blood. If he didn't find help soon, murderous determination or not, he wouldn't make it.

Stratos dare not look at any other part of his body. But then he could not look anywhere else in his crumpled up prison. Wherever he looked there was a reminder of what he used to be, mainly because there was a part of him that had glooped to the inner walls of the pod.

And yet something didn't seem right.

This wasn't Earth.

Although the sun shone down upon him, the air temperature inside the capsule was perishingly cold. Where had he landed? Was this some kind of ice moon! He had been so perturbed by his new injuries that he had failed to notice the snowflakes cascading down into the pod where he lay. In fact, not only was the snow falling inside the capsule, it was starting to flood it.

With great effort, and agony, Stratos tried to move his right arm a few inches towards a bank of buttons. With this effort came even more pain. After all that he had been through, it was a miracle that he was still alive let alone able to move a few inches to the right!

The snow continued to flow heavily into the pod. Around where his ankles used to be, pools of snow began to form, stained red in places where bits of Stratos should have been.

With one final effort, on the verge of unconsciousness again, he threw everything he had at the button and pressed it firmly. A little red light blinked on and off in its place and with that, Stratos blacked out.

Outside the pod, an even bigger light began to blink in and out of existence. And not far away, someone had noticed…

*

'Sir, miss, I think you should come and take a look at this.'

Jake and Anji, the latter still changing into a fresh set of jeans and a jumper, pounded out of their living quarters and towards the cockpit at the front of the Venus II.

There they found Skateboard at the controls of the ship in the space that was normally occupied by Random as the main pilot.

'Look on the screens,' he instructed.
On the scanner was an outline of what looked like an asteroid, only with a large complex built into it.

'The Valetudinarium,' Jake read aloud. 'What's that when it's at home then?'

'It's a hospital. The most comprehensive hospital this arm of the galaxy'.

'By comprehensive, do you mean best?' asked Anji.

'For what Random needs, yes,' said Skateboard.

'Let's go there then!' cried Anji. 'Step on the pedal, Skateboard.'

'It's a long way away, miss, and we haven't got the reserves to get us there.'

'So what, we need fuel?' asked Jake.

'Precisely,' said Skateboard.

They both looked out of the cockpit's windows.

'Where?' asked Anji. There was not a moon, no planet, not even a nebula anywhere near them. No sign of life in sight.

'Roughly 70 clicks away. We have enough to get there, but one of us will have to go outside and...er...fill her up, as it were.'

'A space petrol station?' laughed Anji. 'Don't we need money?'

'Not if we have a wounded person in our party, no,' replied Skateboard.

Anji rushed out of the cockpit.

'Where are you going?' asked Jake.

'To get my spacesuit.'

'What's the rush, we've got 70 clicks to go.'

'I know but I want to be prepared.'

'Can we hyper drive there, Skateboard?' asked Jake.

'That is with hyper speed taken into account, sir,' chirped Skateboard. 'If you fill up the ship to the brim, miss, we won't need to refuel again for another year.'

'Right gotcha,' she replied from within her quarters.

'Oh, and Anj?' said Jake.

Anji popped her head around the mid-section door, spacesuit half on. 'Yes?'

'You couldn't get me some Haribo while you're at it, could you?'

The space-walk was precarious for a girl from Earth who had never spacewalked before. Anji had taken a deep breath, consuming the last amount of air from the ship's oxygen systems before her helmet started pumping through what she needed for her journey and closed her eyes. As the airlock door hissed open, she felt gravity ebb away from right under her feet. Slowly, she began to drift outside.

'Just breathe normally, miss,' came Skateboard's voice over the intercom, pumping communication into a speaker either side of her ears.

'Okay, I can do this...I can do this,' she chanted to herself. With one small push off the edge of the airlock doors, Anji took a giant leap and became the first hu-man being to venture into space to fill up for petrol.

The sensation of floating aimlessly in the dark void was like nothing she had ever experienced before. It was indescribable.

'What's it like?' Jake asked.
'It's amazing!' Anji marveled as she turned around and saw the airlock door shut. 'I feel...light!'

Skateboard took over the comm. 'Okay, Anji, just re-member what I told you. You will find the fuel valve under the port side wing. Can you see it?'

Anji turned to her left. 'Yes, I think I can see it.'
'Good,' said Skateboard. 'Now key in the co-ordinates zero-two-three-mark-five-nine-A into your wrist pad. The suit shall do the rest.'

Anji did just that. Suddenly her body shifted and little hydraulic tubes shot some kind of gas out of the spacesuit and propelled Anji at a gentle pace towards the valve.

Within moments, she was there.
'I'm here! Ooh, this is fun!'
Jake tutted ruefully. *I wish I'd had a go now,* he thought to himself. Although he was braver than he

looked, Anji's appetite for adventure was always greater, even if it had waned slightly after her ordeal back on Genocia with the Mutts in the wastelands. There was no doubting it, although things hadn't quite gone to plan on their last adventure, at least the old Anji was returning back to him.

She proceeded to unscrew the valve and then, using coordinates again commanded over the intercom from Skateboard, propelled herself across the forecourt.

As intergalactic petrol stations go, this one wasn't the glitz and glamour she had expected to find. In fact, it was just as dingy and basic as some of those that adorned the side of motorways back on Earth. Only this one was in space and instead of old Ford Fiestas well past their best, ready for the scrap heap and being driven by teenagers who thought they owned the road but in reality had only just passed their tests, this one has spaceships.

Anji maneuvered to the pump and noticed that there were three options of fuel.

'Er, Skateboard which one do I go for?'

'Five Star.'

Anji tutted. 'Bleeding obvious when you think about it.' She lifted the pump and again, using coordinates from Skateboard, began heading back towards the Venus II.

All of a sudden, Anji came to a grinding halt. Something was stopping her from moving towards the ship.

It was almost like she was being anchored back to the pump.

'Anj, what's the matter?' cried Jake.

'Er, sorry guys, you're not going to like this,' she said, 'but you're going to have to move the ship closer. We've parked too far away from the pump!'

A slight adjustment later and Anji was away. She watched as the clock display on the pump spun to full capacity.

'There we are, Skateboard,' she said, making sure the drip at the end of the hose fell within the fuel chamber, 'All done!'

There was no reply.

'Skateboard?'

Still nothing.

Anji looked up at the cockpit, where Jake was mouthing to her that they could not hear her. He pointed to the sign on the wall of the petrol station. It read:

DO NOT USE COMMUNICATION LINKS WHILE FUELING.

'Oh,' Anji gave her friends a thumbs up, replaced the fuel nozzle, screwed the cap on the Venus II and went over to the kiosk.

She floated up to the kiosk operator, who looked as cheerful as a funeral in winter and pressed a button on her chest. Her external speaker system cracked into life.

'Only 16,000 gallons of fuel to declare.'

The creature on the other side of the glass didn't change its expression.

'And?' it replied.

'Well, we've got a sick person on board who needs urgent medical help, so my friend told me we had to declare how much we'd-'

'I can see how much you have used on my system thank you very much,' it said grumpily.

Anji frowned. The creature looked like someone had shaved an otter and had dressed in a company shirt and hat.

The kiosk runner looked down at its screen and then up again.

'Actually, my monitor is playing up, so could I have that amount again please?'

Anji rolled her eyes.

'16,000 gallons.'

'And you're exempt because you are carrying a wounded being on your craft?'

'Well, we are, aren't we?'

'Do you have proof that you have said being in your travelling party?'

'What? No?'

'Well how can I believe you then?'

'He's hardly going to come out, blow a kiss and dance a jig now is he?' she said in an exasperated tone. 'He's in a coma.'

The creature gave out a long and hard sigh. Slowly, it flipped a switch.

'Would the craft in bay 5 please confirm its status?' Anji waited and waited and waited for a response until a blip came from the dashboard in the kiosk.

'Oh,' said the attendant, 'He does look ill.'

'They sent you a photo?!'

'Yes, that proves it. Hold on I'll write you a receipt.'

'Quickly, if you please?'

'Hold on, I'll get a pen.'

Anji was beginning to get exasperated.

'You're enjoying this, aren't you?'

'I'm a petrol station attendant. Of course I am enjoying it.'

Anji shot the creature a look of disgust.
'So you're happy to leave someone dying just to alleviate your boredom!?'

'No, actually it's just nice to have someone to talk to.'

'Well hurry up and get a different bloody job!' The attendant sighed again. Anji got the impression he did that a lot.

'I'm a Tamorian. We Tamorians are born and bred for one thing in life. That's to be petrol station kiosk attendants. Now ask yourself, who is the lucky one? Him, or me?'

The attendant scribbled on a piece of paper, ripped it off and handed it to Anji who accepted it gladly.

'Thanks,' she spat. She grasped the paper in one hand and punched the coordinates back to the ship with the other. As she drifted back towards the airlock of the Venus II, she glanced down at the incomprehensible scribbling of the galaxy's worst petrol station attendant and made out four words of the appalling handwriting.

HAVE A NICE DAY.

3

REBORN

He blinked his eyes open. Although his new surroundings were as dark and dingy as the deepest well in the universe, his eyes still strained. He forced them shut again and moaned; anticipating that now he was conscious that wave upon wave of agony was to follow.

But it didn't.

The pain was gone.

So was almost every sensation. He couldn't feel a thing! What had happened to him?

Stratos lay on the cold slab confused and alone, unable to move. He grunted, trying to force his limbs into life, but they just would not move.

He tried again but not one part of his body flinched an inch.

Stratos was paralysed.

He breathed heavily and tried to look at his surroundings, only managing to turn his head left and
right. He was unable to move his chin closer to his
chest to take a gaze at his body, not that he especially
wanted to in this instance. The image of how it looked in
the escape pod was enough to haunt him for the rest of his
life.

'I thought I heard you wake up,' said a voice.
'Who are you? Where are you? Where am I?' he demanded.

'I could ask you the same question.'

'If I told you, you wouldn't believe me.'

'Same,' she retorted. She got up and lent over her
patient.

'What makes you say that?' said the stranger. 'Are you
a celebrity of some sort?'

'You could say that,' said Stratos, 'Why can't I
move?'

The stranger pulled up a stool from her work bench and
sat beside her patient.

'I am Professor Garben. You're on an unnamed
moon and you are unable to move because...well, I'm not
sure how to break this to you-'

'Tell me!' demanded Stratos. There followed a brief
silence. 'Please,' he continued.

Garben shot him a concerned look.
'I'm so sorry but...your body was badly damaged by the
crash. When I intercepted your distress signal, it

took me an hour to dig you out and when I found you...' she stopped herself, remembering the horror of what she had found, '...Well, there wasn't much of you left. I stabilised you, the ice had done well to preserve what it could in such a short space of time, but it wasn't enough. It kept you alive until you got back here to my workshop but from then on I'm afraid I had to do anything I could to keep you alive.'

Stratos was starting to fear the worst.
He took short, shallow breaths mustering the effort to ask his next question.

'So...what have you done to me then?'

'You must remember that what I have done was purely a measure to prolong your existence.'

Garben couldn't get the words out. She fumbled around for a mirror in her pocket. In a twisted way, maybe showing him would be easier to comprehend than her telling him.

She produced the small mirror and thrust it in the face of her patient.

Stratos' eyes widened in horror.

His body was gone.

There was nothing left of him from the neck down. 'I'm sorry. Your body was broken, diseased. It couldn't sustain your life any longer. I had to dispose of it. I did the best I could, but there is a solution.'

Stratos was lost for words. All gone, his entire body had been thrown away, probably burnt. Nothing left except his head.

'H-h-how…' he struggled to speak.
Garben got up off the stool and walked over to a bank of complex, important looking instruments.

'These computers are the only thing that's keeping you alive right now. Although your brain is intact, un-damaged, these are doing the rest for you. Even though you may think that you are breathing, there is a tube running from here into your brain to keep it pumping with oxygen. Your motor neuron senses are still working, hence why you are awake. But you will feel no pain currently.

I have turned down your pain receptors. So although you have nothing to feel pain, the brain is such a vital component in the body that it can play all sorts of tricks on you.'

Stratos' mouth was dry. He was still reeling from the shock. Who wouldn't be in the circumstances? But there was more he needed to know.

'Why did you keep me alive?'
'Because it is against my code, my nature to leave someone like that. I might be exiled but I am still a doctor. If there is a chance of life, any chance, I have to take it.'

'Look, I don't want your life story. Please, tell me, what are you going to do to me?'

Garben moved back onto her stool.

'It's entirely up to you. I'm a doctor of medicine first but I am also a Professor of electronics and augmented reality. So I am fully qualified to reconstruct your body, although being a long way away from my usual tools I can still build you something that might be crude but enough to prolong your life, if that's what you want?'

'Of course!'

'Forgive me, I know I sound curt but this is a big choice that you must make. I've worked with implants throughout my career, replaced bits of bodies with exact replicas of what people had before, improved them even! But for someone to be given a completely new body, something which isn't their own, well, it can cause all kinds of trauma.'

'Listen-'

'Garben.'

'Listen, Garben, I am just a head. This is a living nightmare. I don't want to be a floating brain in a jar. I want to be able to move again, to be free of pain. Your proposal is a godsend. I'd appreciate it greatly if you could construct me a new body.'

'But you're not listening. I am trying to tell you that what I can do for you is make you a crude bio metric mode of transport. It won't look anything like your old one. I don't have my full capacity here in this workshop and we are planets away from anyone who can help with supplies.'

'So what you're saying is that I will look more robot than man?'

'Precisely.'

Stratos mulled the proposition over. He could be capable of almighty power, impervious to pain and damage. What wasn't there to like about that idea? It was a great upgrade on the fallible flesh he had been born with.

He had made up his mind.

'Good.'

*

As Garben set about her work, far away on the edge of the remote, barren galaxy that the moon that Stratos had been marooned upon, a nondescript, insignificant little scavenger craft had just entered the long forgotten backwater of space known as the Falovarian system.

The Falovarian system is renowned by astronomers the galaxy over as being unique among many star systems in the universe for one simple reason.

There are no planets, only moons.

But their research was never broadcast amongst the population of surrounding systems because for one reason. The dark section of space was used to banish those who had broken laws in the local sectors of the galaxy and whose punishment wasn't to be as harsh as death, although some would have wished it upon themselves rather than a lifetime of isolation on desolate plains.

There were small crumbs of comfort for the exiles, however. Although some decreed that this was a futile method of punishment, others found it truly inspiring. Depending on the length of sentence, after the exile had served their sentence, they and all their belongings were simply beamed back to where they lived. The prisoners, as it were, were given food replicators, that if broken could be fixed remotely by hard light holograms transported across the stars from the safety of their offices, so that they would not come to any harm. The moons all had breathable atmospheres too and although some ecosystems were...unpredictable...to say the least, they were ultimately livable. That was down to the lack of surrounding planets, the scientists who were integral to the exile programme had explained.

It was entirely possible for the weather to be both sunny and cold at the same time. So it could snow whilst also feeling like a warm Spring day or the sun could be blazing down but it could feel colder than the metal that was currently being sculpted around what remained of Stratos' windpipe. It had a maddening effect on the exiles unfortunate enough to live out their sentences in solitude.

However, they were afforded small luxuries. For some, that meant books, a life supply of hard drives stuffed full of their favourite entertainment or in Garben's case, a small workshop to continue on her experiments. Although she was a Cybernetic surgeon, her exile was completely unrelated to her work and so, she was afforded her wish that her workshop and all that was in it, was transported to the nameless moon that had been her home for the past two months.

And in that time, despite her long treks across the boring, tedious looking rock that Garben had been left upon, she had never come across another living soul.

But she was not alone.

And now, someone was coming to be rescued. Samlore Charbok had said nothing to anybody for

four years. In that time, he had barely left his chair. He had sat patiently waiting, passing the time recounting his former glories. The cultures he had pulped. The pi-rates left ravaged by his hand. He had been captured and tried following a sting operation led by the Sirus Police Corps and his punishment instead of death, for nothing else than Judge and Jury had wanted him to suffer a lifetime of solitude, instructed that he be imprisoned on the moon for life.

He chuckled as the sentence was carried out. He knew it would only be a matter of time before they found him. Any moment now, his crew would be here. It had taken them a long time, but he knew. He just knew.

He pressed his hands into his long, untamed beard. Even for a Samlore - a race of scavengers affectionately dubbed the vermin of the universe by those who they pillaged - his patience had been commendable. Samlores were not well renowned for their patience. If they got bored, they'd strip the scalp from the heads of those who opposed them with their long, nail like talons and flew off into the unknown for another race to steal from.

They were space pirates of the worst kind.
They would always leave a gruesome reminder of who they were when they had fled the scene of a conquest.

Which left a distinguishable trail for the Space Corps to follow and eventually they were caught.

However over a few years they had rebuilt their rabble piece by piece and now they were coming back to claim their Captain.

Aboard the ship, a group of repulsive Salmores were gurgling out their victory cry like a band of rowdy football fans after winning a cup final. Only with more head butting. The Salmores were an abhorrent race of creatures. Their skin was a putrid green, with the slimy texture of a frog, although anyone who had got close enough to one of them to discover this hadn't lived long. Their eyes were small and narrow and were close to their pig-like snouts, which drooled with unmen-tionable regularity and two huge tusks protruded upwards from their bottom gums.

On top of their skulls bore long swathes of fatty skin that seemed to dribble over their heads like long hair and their stomachs wobbled over their armoured trousers, with their legs bent and long like a horse born backwards.

Two things were well established in the galaxy when it came to Samlores.

One - they were not to be messed with.

Two - they were never going to win any Best Looking competitions.

Luckily for the Samlores, they only really cared about one of these things...and pretended not to be hurt about the other.

'Commander,' hollered a Samlore above the ruckus. The Commander, who was only distinguishable from his crew by his sash of sharp weapons he wore over his shoulder, pushed through the crowd. One of the crew was forced flat against the cramped craft's internal wall and hit his head on a large pipe. He shook his concussion and ignored the gash in the back of his head and went back to celebrating violently with the rest of his comrades.

'Have you located the Captain?' the Commander growled. Samlores gurgled as they spoke, making it sound like they were perpetually trying to gargle salt water.

'We have,' snarled the pilot.

'Excellent...' cried the Commander. He turned to his crew and reached for his laser sword that was fastened to his belt. With careless forethought of where he was jabbing it, he slashed it into the ceiling and the explosion of sparks garnered the attention of the noisy ramble.

'We've done the impossible,' he grinned. 'We've escaped the harshest prisons in the galaxy, we've found the Falovarian system, it's taken a long time but we've done what many have only ever dreamed of doing. And when we go down there and rescue our Captain, we shall be unstoppable again!'

The crew cheered in unison.
'Right, take us into land!'

*

'Are you ready?'
Garben had worked hard and fast on Stratos' new body. He had been quite impressed by her skills. In reality, she had been sitting on a prototype robot for quite some time. It had been transported with her from her home but she had never got round to finishing off the head, which was odd, considering the head was something so complicated, so fiddly, that many cybernetic experts started on that part first. But she'd always found the actual body to be a good starting post. As she continued to weld Stratos' organic flesh

to the frame, she did wonder whether he would be happy with what she had done. The robot that had formed the basis for this new body was constructed for strength and intimidation. She had planned to use it to rampage intergalactic bank vaults for her. After all, how was she going to continue to finance her cybernetic experiments?

However, on her last raid, which had unfortunately resulted in two workers being killed in the process, her exile had put her work on the robot on hold.

She had to live with the guilt of her actions, and had been doing so well in her isolation. How was she to know how much Nitro 7 to use in that large bank? And more fool the workers for finding it and being to choose when the explosion went off. That's how she'd come to terms with the guilt.

She'd blamed it on others.

As the final nerve endings were connected to the bio skeleton, she marveled at the work that she had done. Even the work on his eyes, which Stratos had complained were not functioning properly. Upon gouging them out, a practice so much easier when the pain receptors of the patient had been switched off, she'd realised that Stratos' optical ends were severely damaged and he would be blind within months.

She'd also been surprised at how unnerved her patient had been during the whole procedure.

Especially when he had refused to be put to sleep.

It was slightly unnerving that Stratos had wanted to be awake the whole time, especially when his eyes were pulled out.

She decided that upon reactivation of his new body, his strength ability would have to be turned to a minimum. She was still unsure who this man really was and it was only by the good nature of her heart, the bits she had left anyway after the accident that caused those deaths, that she hadn't left him for dead. Anyone in her shoes would do the same, wouldn't they? To save a life. Who knows, saving one might mean that she might be able to sleep at night again. Maybe her conscience would let her off.

But only if this man wasn't as dangerous as she was starting to believe.

Who in their right mind would want to stay awake during such an ordeal?

Come to think of it, what kind of man would survive the injuries he was suffering from in the first place?

No, the strength dial must be kept to a minimum.

Especially if she was to spend the rest of her sentence with this man.

Not man...machine.

With a final few tweaks, Garben was finished with her work and stepped back, returned the soldering gun to the workstation and stared at what she had done.

'My eyes...I cannot see.'

The voice was electronic and organic in equal measure.

Garben moved over to the instrument bank.

'Switching optical on...now.'

A flash of light burst into Stratos' view.

'Switching over to independent life support too.' A row of complex hydraulics inside Stratos' new chest heaved up and down, pumping oil and other essential liquids around his new body, lubricating his innards and making sure that vital components would function correctly.

'Switching independent movement to you, now.'

Another switch was flipped and Stratos' new fingers began to move freely.

Stratos grinned. He could feel again. And not just the sensations he could before, they were heightened. He could tell the density of the slab he had been lying upon just by sheer touch.

He was without pain flooding through his body. The feeling of sheer agony and torture had gone. It was replaced with a feeling of strength, robustness, impervi-ous to pain and suffering.

Wait until the universe got a load of him.

Pleased with her work, Garben was starting to feel slightly alarmed by what she had created.

'I must stress, please, it's all I have to work with right now.'

Stratos detected a level of anxiety in her voice.

'The mirror. Give me the mirror.'

Hesitantly, Garben picked up her mirror. She noticed that her hands were shaking. As her trembling fingers passed the mirror into Stratos' huge mechanical hand she retracted quickly and clenching her fists tight, dug her fingers into her palms. She was clammy with fright.

Stratos, with his new eyes in sharp focus, gazed into the little mirror and was alarmed by what he saw.

'How much of me survived the accident?'

Garben gulped. 'About 12% of your body mass.'

'Well, Garben,' he sat up, his new body clanging against the metal slab and swinging his new legs over onto the floor. His feet clapping the ground as he hurled his body weight upright now for the first time, towered over his helper.

His full height must have been nearly nine feet tall.

His new eyes, cold and unblinking glared down at her.

'I'd say that this is a 100% improvement,' he smiled through sharp, metallic teeth. Garben, unable to take her gaze off the incredible feat that she had achieved, began to slip to the floor, quivering in fear.

'Don't be afraid,' he cooed. 'I will not harm you. You have given me life again. Thanks to you, I am reborn.'

The sound of metal echoed around the workshop as he moved about, getting a sense of how this new body worked.

'What can this new thing do?'

Garben picked herself up, reassured at Stratos' word, but still terrified and fascinated in equal measure at her creation and propped herself up on the stool.

'Erm,' she recomposed herself. 'The body that you now have has the capacity to be ten times stronger and ten times faster than the average humanoid life form.'

Stratos, his back to Garben, grinned maniacally.

'Perfect. Just what I needed.'

Picking his hand up, he looked at it and made a fist. 'I don't suppose you mind me taking it for a try out?'

'W-where?'

'Oh, I don't know, outside perhaps?'

He crouched down to fit through the door and tried to open it. Gently, his fingers enveloped the handle and he pulled down to open it.

Nothing happened.

Stratos tried again.

Still nothing.

'What is happening?' he said through gritted teeth. 'Am I malfunctioning?'

'No,' Garben stuttered.

Stratos turned to face her. He stood in shadow, out of the lighting that bled from the ceiling over the slab that Garben had worked on.

The image was the stuff of nightmares.

'Then what have you done?' he hissed. 'I just wanted to be safer than sorry...'

Before Garben had a chance to explain further, the sound of rockets pierced the still air. The noise grew louder and louder.

Garben rushed to the window and looked outside. There in the snow, was a small ship coming in to land.

'That's impossible,' gasped Garben.

'What is?' asked Stratos.

'This is an exile moon. No-one should be able to find it.'

'And yet, someone has,' said Stratos. He went over to the same window and crouched down to see for himself.

The ship had landed roughly one hundred feet away, but with his telescopic vision, Stratos could make out a side door sliding open.

Suddenly, he recoiled as to his horror, a pack of Samlores began to spill out of it and laser swords primed, proceeded to charge towards the workshop.

'Garben, you must turn off my strength inhibitor.'

'Why?'

'Don't argue, just do it!' he yelled.

Garben jumped to it, clambering to the instrument bank. She flicked a couple of switches and instantly, Stratos began to feel the strength grow within his new body.

Without warning, a blaster bolt shot through the window, sending Garben scrambling to the ground. The shot embedded itself in the instruments on the wall, blowing any chances of the inhibitors from limiting Stratos now. There was another bolt at the other end of the workshop. Bits of broken glass lay strewn across the slab. Stratos was unmoved.

Suddenly, the Samlores burst in through the door. They immediately stopped as soon as they clapped eyes on the terrifying machine that stood, unafraid, in front of them.

'Hold your fire!' came a cry from the front. Stratos glared down with murderous intent at the dozen or so Samlores who stood quaking before him.

'You only needed to knock,' he said calmly.

'Samlores like to make an entrance,' said the lead Samlore.

'Who am I addressing?' asked Stratos.

'Samlore Charbok, Captain of the Dangoza.' Stratos looked over their shoulders, which was easy for him given his new head for heights, and looked upon their little ship with utter contempt.'

'What? That little thing?'

'That hunk of junk is not mine, never has been, we shall liberate the Dangoza from the Space Corps.'

'So why are you bothering us then?'

'Well, before I escape this hole of a moon once and for all, we Samlores thought we should do what we do best...scavenge.'

'Well there's nothing here for you to scavenge,' said Stratos.

'Oh yeah? Says-'
Charbok was halted by something cold and powerful gripping his throat. Soon he seemed to be levitating in mid-air. The Samlores remained unmoved, petrified to the spot.

Stratos had picked up the Captain of the Samlores like he was a rag doll. He held him up close to his face. Charbok tried kicking and hitting with all his might, but he had dropped his weapon when he was grabbed. Stratos began to squeeze.

'Says me…'said Stratos. With a terrible blood curdling squelch, Charbok was no more and Stratos hurled his body clean out of the door, passed the stunned Samlores and off into the distance.

The Samlores instantly laid down their weapons and dropped to the floor, begging to be spared.

Stratos laughed.
'You pitiful beings need a new Captain...I accept the position.'

The Samlores agreed in unison, still pleading not to be hurt.

'Silence!'
They all stopped instantly.
'Let's go...you are in my command now and anyone who disagrees can rest uneasily that they will not be breathing for long.'

The Samlores began to file out of the workshop. Before he left, he looked over at Garben, who had propped herself underneath the slab.

'I owe you my life, Garben. In return I spare yours.' Garben, tears running down her face, brought up the courage to speak.

'Who are you?'

Stratos smiled.

'I am Stratos. Destroyer of Worlds.'

And with that, Stratos left.

Garben, still shaking severely, slowly left the confines of her shelter and crawled across the broken glass to the door.

By the time she had reached it, the craft doors were shutting and the tiny scavenger ship was ready to leave.

'Oh god,' said Garben as she watched the ship take off. 'What have I done?'

4

THE VALETUDINARIUM

Random awoke from a fever dream in a very strange place indeed. At least, he thought it was a fever dream. Or maybe it was his recollection of events, strange as they were, that led him to feel so...weak? He took a sharp intake of breath and listened to the noises around him. The intermittent beeping and the coughing, the sound of professionals tending to others. Then there was the sickening smell of a sterilised atmosphere. From that alone he deduced that he was in some kind of hospital, but where?

Why and almost as equally as important, how?' He felt cold...and yet hot at the same time. His body hurt and ached like nothing he had ever felt before.

Random wondered why.

He started to dig deep back into his mind to work out what had happened to him.

It all seemed to happen so...quickly.

At first, things had gone swimmingly, then less so. He remembered Spectronia and that immense power of the Zedron Flux. He recollected the ultimatum he had to give to the Osirons to stop them from blowing up the planet.

And then...did he?

His blood ran cold.

He had, hadn't he?

He'd activated the Flux to destroy an entire race.

Genocide.

'Skateboard, he's stirring!' came a cry from a familiar voice.

It was Anji. He could feel her holding his hand. Or was that the other one? Jake? No, it wasn't Jake. The person who was holding onto him smelt too nice to be Jake.

With extreme caution, Random began to open his eyes and instantly regretted his decision.

The blinding white lights of his hospital cubicle made them water.

'Random, buddy, you're back!' came another voice. Random shut his eyes again and decided to use another of his senses to conclude who this new voice belonged to.

He sniffed the air. The sterile was joined by an over-whelming level of anti-perspirant.

It was Jake alright.

'Please, don't crowd him,' came another, less familiar tone.

'He's going to be okay, right?' Jake spoke again.

Random wanted to assure him he would be fine, he really did, but when he tried to speak his throat was so dry it felt like someone had poured an entire desert into it.

'He needs to rest,' came the stranger's voice again.

And with that, Random fell back to sleep.

He awoke again sometime later. This time, he felt stronger, less weak.

Daring to open his eyes again, he felt a great sense of relief when, to his great surprise, the overwhelming lights that blinded him before were gone. With caution, he gently levered himself upright but feeling a sudden dizziness, slumped back onto the bed.

He huffed, his breath rapid as though he were ex-hausted after a long run.

'Sir?'

Random's eyes opened again. He certainly knew that mechanical voice.

'Skateboard,' he croaked. His lips were like sandpaper. Licking them and clearing his throat, he said the name of his faithful friend again.

'It's good to have you back with us,' Skateboard sounded relieved, even for a computer. 'For a while we thought there might be no way back.'

So many questions and yet, Random wasn't sure if he wanted to know the answers to any of them.

'Why? Where have I been?' he joked.

'How much do you remember, sir?'

Random sighed. 'Everything.'

'You remember the Flux?'

'How can I forget. I remember what I did. What I had to do. I take it that it nearly killed me?'

'Well, to be precise, sir, the aftershock of the energy the Flux generated has polluted the cells in your body to such an extent that they have been incapable of regenerating, as they would if you broke your leg, for example, to give you sufficient time to heal. So your body was starting to shut down.'

'You could have just said, "yes", Skateboard,' sighed Random.

He fell back in his bed and gazed upward at the ceil-ing. It was very tall, with large chandeliers of lights dangling from metallic beams metres above him.

'What is this place?' asked Random.

'You are in the Valetudinarium,' replied Skateboard.

'Where's that then?'

'Sector 4A of the Hollister System. The biggest hos-pital in the known galaxy. We are on the largest asteroid on a belt surrounding the planet Fro.'

'Hospital...good,' Random said to himself. 'Anji and Jake, they are here, yes?'

Skateboard looked to the side of the bed. Anji was fast asleep in the visitor's chair situated next to Random's sick bed. Her coat had slipped off her sleeping frame and fallen to the floor, so Skateboard produced his inner claws to tenderly put it over her again so as not to wake her.

'They've barely left your side,' said the AI robot.

'I think I can tell,' said Random, suddenly feeling a heavy weight lying across his ankles. It was Jake. He was snoring softly curled up at the foot of the bed.

Random allowed himself a chuckle.

'I've done a terrible thing, old friend. I don't deserve to have survived this.'

Skateboard got up onto his two hind wheels and lined his vision interface level with Random. He was looking upward, his mind in a very distant place.

'You made a decision. A terrible decision that saved the lives of millions.'

'I know but-'

'The Osirans,' Skateboard interrupted, 'Would have ripped the whole planet apart with the Armageddon beam. Destroying all life, including ours in the shock wave. They would then have taken the Flux for their own and destroyed countless lives, countless worlds if you had not done what you did. There's a blessing and a curse being the saviour of Rodas. Sometimes you must take action that others simply cannot. On this occasion, it was a blessing that you were there to do the right thing.'

Random smiled, tears collecting in the corners of his red/blue eyes. He reached out his hand, which he noticed was quivering as the various tubes and drips jangled out of them and patted Skateboard affectionately.

'Sometimes I do wonder where I would be without you, Skateboard.'

'Only sometimes?' the robot joked.

Random smiled. He would live with his decision. Just like he lived with the guilt of blowing up Anji and Jake's school and condemning the Sandman to the fire. Like he had done when liberating Genocia.

Like he did, day after day, to not go back to Rodas and meet his destiny.

'If sir does not mind my saying so, I think you should get some rest. Your test results come back to-morrow.'

'Of course not.' Random returned his hand to his side, kicked his ankles that were quickly going dead from underneath the sleeping Jake and very quickly fell back into a deep, dreamless sleep.

*

Meanwhile in another part of space altogether, the little scavenger ship sailed away from the prison system Stratos had found himself in with a new Captain at the helm. Stratos had to admit to himself, as he stooped inside the tin can of a vessel, it had been incredibly easy for him to take charge.

But what he was unaware of was that the Samlore race was, despite their devious, violent nature, quite cowardly and pitiful. They are also loyal until they are conquered, at which point they will turn their loyalty to those who have conquered them.

Stratos smiled. They were perfect for his plans.

'O' Great One,' said the Commander to Stratos as he returned from the cockpit.

'No,' said Stratos, 'Supreme Leader is what you will call me.'

The Commander's heart started beating that little bit faster.

'Excuse me,' he saluted.

Stratos grinned. He liked that.

'What do we do now?'

'We need to find a ship. A battle cruiser with the capacity of immense weaponry.'

The Commander moved back into the cockpit and barked the order at his navigator.

'Got one,' said the navigator, who due to his poor sight was wearing what appeared to Stratos as someone else's glasses. Someone he had killed, perhaps.

'Supreme Leader,' said the Commander, gesturing at the scanner screen.

Stratos squeezed into the confined space, jamming not only the Commander and navigator in with him, but also the pilot and another Samlore who seemed to carry out no other function but to serve drinks. As he realised that he was now trapped in the cockpit with everyone else, he awkwardly perched on the end of a chair.

Stratos gazed at the scanner and witnessed a large blob blip in and out of existence on the top left hand corner of the screen.

'The only ship within range with weaponry is the Orbital, 12 clicks away.'

'Then set a course, it's ours.'
The Commander's jaw slackened and the tea boy dropped the foul smelling liquid in the goblet to the floor.

'Supreme Leader…'whispered the Commander, 'The Orbital is one of the mother ships of the Space Seal Corps. It's the most heavily guarded space carrier in the sector. There's no way we can take it-'

'We can and we shall,' Stratos interrupted.
'But...why?' the Commander dared to ask. 'To
send a message,' said Stratos coldly.

*

'Welcome back to the land of the living!' Anji enthused.

It was the following morning and Random was still finding his strength but was at least now able to sit up in bed, no matter how many tubes and drips were anchoring him to the spot.

'Morning to you too,' he quipped.

'How are you feeling, buddy?' yawned Jake.

'I'd be lying if I said I was back to my normal self,' he replied.

Jake fished about the end of the bed for something. 'Well if you fancy some breakfast...here you go!' he said, producing a brown bag and handing it to his friend.

Now he came to mention it, Random was famished. It felt like a lifetime ago since he had eaten. Had food even passed his lips when he was on Spectronia?

He dived into the bag and pulled out a bunch of half-eaten, browning grapes.

Random bulked. 'On second thoughts, I'll skip breakfast.'

'Well, I suppose I did buy them a week ago...and I got hungry on the way back from the shop.'

Random's ears pricked up. 'A week ago?! I've been in here a week?!'

'You've been asleep for a couple of days on top of that,' said Anji.

Random struggled to make this new information process in his fuzzy brain.

'So, what happened?' he asked.

Anji shrugged. 'Don't know. You'd seen off the Osirons and by the time we got to the top of the cliff you'd already started to collapse. Random?' she drew herself closer, 'It couldn't be anything to do with what you were trying to tell me in the cave, could it?'

Random frowned. He had forgotten about the voices in his mind, the incessant consciences that plagued him, told him to go home and fulfill his destiny. He hadn't wanted to saddle Anji and Jake with his worries that they were becoming more frequent because at the end of the day they were only human. They'd never understand. Moreover, he didn't want them to worry. But clearly now the cat was out of the bag.

'No. And don't worry you two, your pilot hasn't started to take leave of his senses.'

'We're not worried about our pilot, mate,' said Jake, who in this time had liberated the bag of week-old grapes back off Random and was quietly scoffing them. 'We're worried about our friend.'

'Well,' said a smiling Random, 'You've no need to worry, I'm getting back to where I need to be. Slowly, but surely.'

'Let's hope you go purple again too, eh?' said Anji absentmindedly.

'Sorry, say that again?' asked Random.

'Oh,' said Anji.

Random began to look around for something, any-thing, that would show his reflection. Jake did the same and as Anji struggled to find her mirror inside her bag, Jake found a metallic pan under the bed and handed it to Random.

Random's eyes grew larger than a planet as he saw for the first time, inside the warped image of his bed pan, that his skin had gone red and blue.

'What the-'

The rude word Random said next was drowned out completely by an announcement over the speaker system.

'WOULD DOCTOR KILDER, DOCTOR MADONEY AND DOCTOR SELBY PLEASE MAKE THEIR WAY URGENTLY TO MATERNITY ROOM 39? FOR EVERYONE ELSE, PLEASE RETURN TO YOUR BEDS. THERE IS NO CAUSE FOR PANIC OR ALARM.'

The intercom clicked off and a few seconds later clicked back on again.

'JUST A MESSAGE TO ALL INPATIENTS AND MEMBERS OF STAFF IF YOU DO HAPPEN TO FIND A SELOPTAN BABY IN ONE OF YOUR WARDS, PLEASE STAY AWAY FROM ITS TENTACLES, ESPECIALLY THE SHARP ONES, UNTIL THE MIDWIVES CATCH UP WITH IT, THANK YOU.'

Of course Random heard none of this. He just stared, lost for words, at his reflection.

Red and blue.

How?

Skateboard made his way into Random's ward, doing his best to stay out of the way of the mixture of patients, doctors and nurses en route back from the Venus II. It was a fairly long walk - the ship had been parked on the western wing of the asteroid since they had landed and Random was on the opposite side of the Valetudinarium, which was not ideal but manageable for Skateboard's daily treks back to Random's bedside. After all, the asteroid was five miles long and two and a half miles across, meaning that although it could be a tiresome trek for Anji and Jake, at least they were all keeping fit.

For the first couple of nights, Skateboard had allowed the pair to sleep by his master's bedside but when the hospital management had begun to take a disliking to this, for space reasons, which was ironic considering how big the hospital was, he had insisted that they begin to go back to the Venus to sleep and eat. He certainly needed to recharge his batteries - a lesson he had learnt the hard way on Spectronia - but then he began to realise that they were sneaking back in the middle of the night.

Originally, he put this behaviour down to their age, acting out and being rebellious against authority perhaps. After all, the Valetudinarium wasn't just a hospi-tal. It was a whole new place to explore. But that didn't stop Skateboard worrying about what kind of infectious diseases or terrible things they might encounter here alone without him.

Yet he needn't have worried. The first morning they had done this, when he had panicked and was just seconds away from alerting the hospital security that his friends were missing, he had returned to Random's bedside and found that they were asleep next to their ill friend.

And so the tradition had continued. Every morning, that's where he would find them. He didn't say any-thing, why would he? He just chirped to himself how lucky Random was that he had two loyal friends.

And how lucky he himself was to have all three of them.

As Skateboard neared Random's ward, dodging a sticky, squelchy looking infant Seloptan baby and the nets that a gaggle of harangued midwives were throwing at it, he whirred over in his mind why his friend had changed colour in his stricken state?

Whatever damage the Flux had done to him, they'd know soon enough, but in the meantime, he would have to break the news to his friend gently.

The ward was a hive of activity. Roughly 30 beds, adorning a multitude of aliens with a range of differing ailments, lined the back wall. The ward was a long tube of clinical equipment and white light. It had struck Anji and Jake when Random was first wheeled into his bay, how much it resembled a hospital back on Earth, barring the futuristic equipment, of course and the incredibly tall ceiling. Skateboard had pointed out to them that wherever the hospital may be, it still needed to serve the same purpose and hence why they all looked so similar.

A Doctor nearly swished his reptilian tail right in the path of Skateboard as he made his way to Random's bed and had it not been for a beep from Skateboard's speaker system to let him know he was there, he'd have been swiped right into the wall.

'Do excuse me,' said the posh Doctor.
'Not a problem, sir,' said Skateboard as he merrily made his way to his master's side.

He whirred to himself, he would have smiled if he had a face, when he saw that Anji and Jake were by his side as always.

'Good morning to you all,' he said in his usual posh manner.

Anji and Jake sat pensively in their places. Random didn't move. Barely blinked.

'Oh my, are you all frozen in time?' he quipped. Then he noticed that Random was looking at his reflection.

'Oh,' he said.
'Skateboard…' Random uttered. 'What? How?'

'We should soon know, your test results arrive back this morning,' he cooed. 'Now please put that down sir, you know where that has been, and try to relax.'

'You're getting your results this morning, Random, I'm sure it isn't permanent,' said Anji, trying her best to allay his worries.

'Unless you prefer it?' Jake said, shrugging his shoulders. 'And who knows? Next planet we go to, red and blue might be in with the season?'

Anji frowned. 'Oh yeah, because you're all about fashion statements Captain Shabby.'

'That's harsh!' said Jake in defence. Although after looking down at his clothes, which hadn't been changed in a few days, maybe she had a point.

Random dropped the bed pan, which made a horrible clunking noise as it fell to the ground and threw himself back onto his pillow.

'Whatever they say, let's hope it's good news.'
'It's bad news, I'm afraid,' said the Doctor, who de-spite the absence of a mouth - or indeed eyes or nose - on her face, somehow managed to convey the test re-sults to Random and his friends audibly.

Jake wondered where the mouth indeed was on the Doctor's body, before quickly thinking it probably wasn't something he should be imagining.

Random shuffled uncomfortably in his bed.

'Okay, hit me.'

'The radiation from the power you were exposed to has damaged your central nervous system, your musculoskeletal system, your metabolism and your skin pigmentation has been compromised. It's fair to say that it is a miracle that you are still alive.'

'So what does this all mean? Is he going to die?' Anji asked, fearing the worst.

'Everyone dies,' remarked the Doctor, in a tone a local butcher would have been proud of. 'But if you get plenty of rest and some drugs from our chemist, your metabolism should begin to repair your body, but I'm afraid it's going to be a slow process. Truly, we have never seen a body as remarkable as yourself. To which species do you belong again? Rodasian, you said?'

'Yes, but for the sake of my patient confidentiality, please do not tell anyone,' Random replied in hushed tones.

'Of course, if you wish,' said the Doctor.

'How long until he can be discharged?' asked Jake. 'Not
for a while yet. Although your body is repairing
it will take a while, like I said, until you are back to normal, if indeed you get there. If you do not rest then your recuperation will be compromised. Even for such a unique individual as yourself, remember you have been in a coma for over a week, time will be the teller. Until then, rest up and relax. I have to complete my rounds now but if there is anything else I can do, let

me know. I'll get onto the pharmacy and see if there is anything we can do to help boost your metabolism.'

'Before you go, Doctor, does this...radiation mean that I've endangered those who I've been in close proximity to since then?'

The Doctor smiled.

'No, your exposure was internal, there is no way that your family have been put at risk. We'll get you started on medication this afternoon. Until then, good day.'

The Doctor slithered away, medical tablet readout in hand.

Random turned back to his friends.

'Family?'

'We had to tell them we were your next of kin,' said Anji.

'So who are you then? My sister?'

'Your wife,' she corrected.

'My Wife?!' said Random before turning to Jake 'And you my Brother?'

'Er...husband actually?'

'What?! Does that make Skateboard my husband too then?'

'Certainly not, sir!' lied Skateboard. 'We had to pretend we were next of kin otherwise they would not have cared for you. So after a little research, we decided that we would say that we were of the faith of the Church of Many and left it there. In that religion you can have up to twelve husbands or wives of your choosing.'

'I bet the divorce rate is insurmountable!' Random remarked.

A short time later, Jake found Anji on the observation deck of the East wing of the Valetudinarium. After Random had returned to sleep, the three of them had gone their separate ways and after a change of clothes, Jake joined Anji's side as she gazed at the planet below.

'Beautiful, isn't it?' she admired.
The planet shone gloriously in the darkness of space. The asteroid belt the Valetudinarium belonged to hung around it like a necklace.

'It sure is,' said Jake, who noticed that Anji's arms were held tightly around herself. 'Hey, don't worry Anj. You heard what they said. He'll be fine.'

'No, they said that he might be. He needs a lot of time to get over this - who's to say that he will be the same when he finally gets over it? Or what long lasting damage that bloody Flux thing has done to him?'

Jake shrugged. 'I suppose we just have to see. What was it the Doctor said? "Time will be the teller?"'

'Very profound,' replied Anji.
'Look, as long as he is here in this hospital resting up then nothing can go wrong can it?'

Almost at the instant that Jake had finished speaking a huge ship blasted past the view screen, making

Anji, Jake and the other dozen or so aliens in the area fall to the floor as it trembled beneath their feet.

'You had to say it!' said Anji as she helped her friend back up to his feet.

'What the hell was that?' asked Jake to nobody in particular.

The pair watched as the ship, a huge battle freighter honed away from the hospital and flew out further into space. A murmur of discontent surrounded them as fellow patients, nurses and next of kin gathered around the glass to get a better look.

The freighter's engines came to an abrupt halt high above the planet below. A loud crackle abruptly pierced through the speaker system all around the hospital.

On the East wing wards, the patients that were asleep, including Random, awoke with a startle. Random pulled himself upright in bed, a hum of something in the atmosphere sparking his attention.

Suddenly, a voice boomed into life.

'Peoples of this system please attend carefully.' The voice was metallic yet organic and malicious. 'I come looking for the one who has dared to put a stop to my galactic conquest. The one who is known to the universe as the bringer of darkness. Random.'

Anji and Jake looked at each other confused and alarmed in equal measure. Elsewhere on the asteroid,

Random and Skateboard, who had returned to his master's bed, did exactly the same.

'Ever heard of him?' came the voice once more. Those who had gathered by the window begin to chatter among themselves.

'Anj, we've got to get him out of here,' said Jake nervously.

'No?' came the voice once more. 'Well, let me leave him a message...'

The tremor became more and more violent as a red light began to shine from underneath the belly of the freighter. It looked hotter and brighter second by second until suddenly with a terrifying finality, a beam of thunder seemed to explode from the huge freighter down upon the planet below.

What happened next was the stuff of nightmares. As the incumbents of the viewing deck were thrown to the floor and the patients on the wards were thrown from their beds, the planet began to split and with sickening finality exploded in a fireball that sent a shock wave of earthquake proportions bursting through the asteroid belt.

Someone on the Valetudinarium must have turned a self-defense shield on the asteroid as debris started to fly towards the hospital and then deflect off an invisible force keeping it out of harm's way.

As the inhabitants of the Valetudinarium, shocked and stunned by what they had just seen, gathered themselves the best they could, a panic began to shriek around the halls of the place. Anji and Jake lay there on the floor, stunned by what they had just witnessed, lost for words.

'I think he got the message,' said the horrible voice once again. 'If he wants to put a stop to all of this...then the purple one will have to find me...'

And with that, in a blinding flash the Freighter went to warp and disappeared, leaving nothing else but a silent, hollow space where the planet, where upon billions of lives had just been lost, was no more.

Anji and Jake, among the chaos surrounding them, turned to each other. Jake looked terrified and managed to break their silence.

'We've gotta get out of here!'

5

SIEGE

The metal monster sat brooding in a tiny corner of the Samlores stolen ship. Waiting. Impatiently.

Revenge for him was best served instantly. Although to him it had only been a few hours since the Commodore had fallen to Random's efforts, with this new body, he wanted to move as swiftly as time would allow him - but time was also an enemy to him right now.

Aligning himself with the Samlores, a pathetic race of snivelling vermin not worthy to lace the space boots of his most trusty loyal soldiers, was nothing short of embarrassing to a man of his great stature.

But they would never have to know - those who had survived of course.

As soon as the Freighter was theirs, which it would be no matter what the Space Seals threw at them,

Stratos would make sure of that and wreak havoc… just as soon as his message to Random had been delivered.

With the knowledge he had within his head, and the might of his new body, as soon as the arsenal of devastation was at his mercy, nothing could stop him.

Not even Random.

He looked down at the two grossly over proportioned fists that sat clenched in his lap. They made a jangling sound as he rested them on his thighs. Well, they were his thighs now. The arms were huge, heavy, dangerous. It was like having two submarines for limbs. But he liked them. His body had been augmented, improved, and it was going to serve its purpose.

The trauma of losing his own body was so minute it didn't bother him. How was he to obtain supremacy with a broken vessel that was no longer worthy of containing his ambitions. This new one served it just so.

The hydraulics that replaced his innards were pumping toxins everywhere, poisonous to anyone else who came into contact with them and keeping Stratos' poisoned mind on the job in hand.

He was starting to get cross.

Why weren't they there yet?

He was yearning to give this new body a test drive. To sample it's destructive force.

Stratos growled loudly, thrust himself upright and marched towards the cockpit, knocking unwitted Samlores aside as he cleared his path.

'Report!' he barked.

The pilot looked nervously over his shoulder.

'We are nearly there, Supreme Leader.'

'Nearly is not now, is it?'

The pilot paused, throwing the question over in his incredibly dense mind.

'Er...no,' he coughed.

Stratos bent down and leered at him.

The pilot stared into his deep, soulless eyes.

'So...how much longer?' Stratos spat, a spray of clear fluid dispersing on the pilot's face.

The pilot gulped. The scavenger ship stuttered to a halt. Stratos glanced up away from the terrified Samlore and took a look through the view screen.

In front of them, a huge vessel swelled over the little craft, blocking out the blackness of space.

'Good,' grinned Stratos. 'I like an efficient pilot. For a moment there I thought I was going to have to kill you,' he said casually, patting the pilot roughly on his shoulder, make the cold sweat pour just that little quicker for the shocked occupant.

'Supreme Leader.'

It was the Commander's weasley voice that broke the silence.

'What are your orders?'

Stratos turned around to face his subjects.

'We get ourselves arrested. And then, as soon as we are aboard, we strike. Who knows? if you're lucky I might let you have some of the fun too. I want the ship, I don't care what you do to the crew, just make sure that they are disposed of. Feel free to get creative.'

The Samlores gurgled in horrible appreciation.

'Crew?' asked Stratos.

'247, Supreme Leader. We are but 12 in number,' said the pilot.

A sickening clash of metal on bone propelled the pilot out of his chair and into a bank of important looking dials and switches on the adjacent wall. The pilot was dead before he hit the ground and as his lifeless form fell to the floor, Stratos retracted his fist.

'I will not stand negativity. It spreads like a disease, infecting unless cured straight away. This freighter may be the size of a small moon, but don't let it intimidate any of you. These ships have a small crew despite their size...we can quell them. You just have to do what I say. Is that clear?'

The Samlores nodded their heads in agreement.
'This is the Orbital. Please state your business in this quadrant.'

The voice came from the ship's communication systems.

'What shall we say?' asked the Commander.
'Nothing,' replied Stratos.
'This is the Orbital. Please respond.'

*

The rookie at the desk clicked the comms button off again. Fresh out of the academy, it was only her second week on board the Orbital. A fortnight out in the real world. It was nothing that she thought it would be.

It was boring.

Her commanding officer, a steel faced, rigid woman twice her age, stood pensive over her shoulder.

'Nothing, Ma'am.'

The commanding officer turned on her heels and paced, hands behind her back.

'How many lifeforms on board?'

'12. Just running a security scan on the ship right now,' said the desk operator.

She surveyed the bridge whilst awaiting the results, large, cavernous, far too big for the crew that she was in charge of. But if they were to maintain the security of the sector, and protect the cargo they had on board, they had to be sure that nothing was compromised.

She turned to the other officers sitting along the long, vast command bank of complex computers and sighed. This was supposed to be her day off. Why did she get the impression it wasn't going to be a quiet one?

'I should have called in sick,' she muttered to no-body in particular.

The scavenger ship was plastered across every single monitor on the bridge. The huge area was a hive of activity, a buzz of electrical instruments hummed in the background as the newbie had finished completing their scans.

'It's stolen, Ma'am.' she confirmed.
The commanding officer leaned back over the desk and peered at the monitor.

'Send a patrol down to Bay 3. Get a tractor beam fixed on that ship. Bring them in.'

The scavenger ship put up no fight as it was dragged into the belly of the Orbital. As it rested on the floor of Bay 3 and as the security patrol surrounded it and cocked their laser guns, the ship itself was silent.

'Hold your positions,' said a voice from under one of the helmets.

The bay was still, like the calm before the storm.
'This is the Orbital. Come out with your hands up,' came another.

Still there was no sign of life.
The patrol seemed unmoved. They had been trained for situations such as this and seen them many times over.

They were happy to wait.
However long it took.
After a few minutes, a creaking sound started to emit from the ship. Within moments, carnage was released.

Without warning, something ripped through the door of the scavenger ship, tearing it's hull away like paper. It leaped out of the hole and with a devastating swipe of its arm wiped a couple of soldiers clean off their feet and across the bay. A volley of laser fire exploded and reverberated around the four walls, as the Samlores began their side of the slaughter.

*

Up on the bridge, an alarm went off instantly. The rookie alerted the commanding officer, who sprung out of her command chair and leapt to her side and watched in horror on the surveillance screen as the carnage unfolded. Her eyes swam in horror as she witnessed a huge cybernetic man rip one of her soldiers to shreds. In all her years of service, she had never seen anything so destructive in one single life form before.

'Seal the bulkhead,' she croaked.
The rookie sprung into action, flicking a number of switches as the bridge crew, snapped out of their shock and back into action.

The Commander made for a cabinet in the wall behind her chair. Pressing a few buttons, the door hissed open, revealing a laser proof vest and a long, shiny laser gun. Fastening the vest over her uniform, she took up arms, closed the cabinet and turned back to the rookie.

'Never call in sick, cadet,' she said.

Stratos had enjoyed the slaughter to such an extent that he had failed to pick up the alarm siren shrieking over the sound of death. As the final corpse slid away from his iron grasp, he surveyed the wreckage. Two Samlores lay slain with their enemy.

'Weak,' said Stratos to his troops. 'We have to get to the bridge. Cut off the snake's head and crush the resistance. Shut off this damn alarm. Follow me.' The Samlores did as they were instructed.

Stratos led them to what should have been the exit out of the bay but a bulk door had slid down to trap them out.

A small hiss of activity could just be heard by Stratos under the sound of the alarm. Soon the Samlores also heard it and started to look around the bay as though they were looking for a swarm of bees buzzing above them.

Stratos turned to see that the bay door that had sealed them inside was starting to slowly open. He growled. They were going to suck them out into space...unless...

Stratos clasped his powerful hands together and started to smash down on the bulkhead. Every blow made a dent and a bone jangling sound as slowly but surely, it was starting to give.

Meanwhile back on the bridge, the commanding officer watched on in terror as she witnessed the monster doing what should have been impossible.

'How long until the bay doors are open?'

The rookie checked her read out.

'Eight seconds.'

She grit her teeth. 'It's not quick enough.'

She was right. The rookie shot a look of panic at her superior.

'Ma'am! He's through!'

As soon as the fists shot through the bulk, a dozen or so troops began firing at them, sending beams of energy ricocheting off Stratos' protected armour.

As the troops began to beg for back up, Stratos' mighty hands tore the bulkhead in two. His army of rogues returned their fire and took out a couple of the Orbital's struggling soldiers. Slowly they forced them back as Stratos ran like a bull into them and allowed his fury to inflict appalling violence against all who stood in their way.

Before long, the corridor they were now standing in fell silent. One of the Samlores was sick as Stratos turned back to his men.

'You!' he pointed at the Commander. 'Find the bridge. Now! We do not split up until the bridge is ours!'

As the Commander made for an info port on the wall another volley of lasers exploded towards them.

Stratos laughed at them as every single shot bounced off him, not even leaving a scorch mark upon him. Even a bolt of fire that was aimed squarely at his head deflected harmlessly away. A force field defence system built into his metallic body was doing it's job.

With lightning pace, Stratos pounced like a jaguar at his prey and the rage surged once more inside of him.

Even though the Commander had found their route to the bridge, they could have just followed the soldier who lay waiting for them like lambs to the slaughter, lining their way to the prize. Stratos pitied them. They never stood a chance.

The commanding officer was at a loss as to what to do next. They were so close now and yet so many of her soldiers, her comrades and more importantly her friends had been sent to their deaths in a futile effort to stop the rampage.

'Ma'am, surely we must abandon!' cried the rookie, who was white with fright.

'No.'

'But Ma'am!' the girl was grappling at the arm of her superior, who stood rigid facing the entrance to the bridge, gun in hand, ready to take on the force of nature that was sure to tear his way inside any moment now.

'Send a distress call to all Space Corps ships in this sector...we can't let them take control, not with what we have on board.'

The rookie tightened her grip on her arm.

'Now!' screamed the commanding officer as she threw the girl to the floor. The girl scrambled to her bank and started to send out the SOS signal.

Behind her, the bridge doors buckled and twisted and before she had a chance to complete the message, she was shot in the back by a bolt from one of the Samlores' guns.

The commanding officer watched as her new officer, fresh with promise and too young to die, fell silently and lifelessly away.

She turned back to face her victor and despite the cold sweat that trickled down her face, kept a lid on the terror she was facing.

Stratos leered over her.

'You are the Captain, yes?'

'I am Admiral Quint of the SSC Orbital and you have committed an act of atrocity that in direct opposition of-'

'Save it!' he demanded. 'Admiral Quint, I hereby relieve you of your services. Order your men to stand down.'

He grabbed her laser gun from her grasp and twisted the barrel until it snapped like a twig. Quint did as she was told and ordered her troops to stand down.

'The Orbital is lost,' she said as she signed off her message.

'Just under new management,' replied Stratos. 'Now Admiral. Run.'

The Admiral looked vaguely at him.

'RUN!' he shrieked.

Again, Quint did as she was told and ran as fast as her legs would carry her out of what used to be the bridge door.

Stratos looked up and saw the multitude of officers who were still on the bridge too.

'You too! Get out! Run away like the cowards that you all are!'

'You heard him, move, move!' barked the Commander as he and the Samlores raised their guns threateningly.

They sprang away from the bridge, knowing that any show of resistance was an instant sentence of death. They'd all seen what had happened in the bay and in the corridors leading up to the bridge.

Resistance was well and truly futile.
As the last Space Seal retreated he was needlessly tripped by the Samlore standing nearest the door. Stratos surveyed all that he had conquered.

'Magnificent...just magnificent...Commander, seal the blast doors.'

The Commander made for the command desk and without hesitation carried out the order. A shutter slid down over the wreckage of the bridge entrance and sealed them in.

'Cut the oxygen to all other levels of the ship.' Coldly, the Commander carried out Stratos' want and in doing so, assured that any resistance stupid enough to try and stop them on the Orbital was soon to be no more. As images of the crew suffocating swam on every monitor within the bridge, the Samlores watched on in dread.

'First they fight like cowards, then they run like cowards and now they die like cowards. How predictable,' quipped Stratos. He moved over towards a bank of instruments further down the line of the Commander. 'Let this be a reminder to you all not to defy me,' he said as he punched in some information into the computer.

'Supreme Leader,' said the Commander who edged closer to him, 'What are you looking for?'

Stratos gave a truly sinister smile.

'This is more than I could have dreamed of,' he cried. 'This freighter has enough weaponry in their cargo, as well as their defence systems to destroy an entire planet.'

The Samlores grinned to one another and gave knowing nods back to Stratos.

'And that's just what we are going to do!' he leered. On a monitor behind him, the image of Admiral Quint gasping for breath stained the monitor before she too succumbed to the inevitable.

'Let's target a neutral world first. Somewhere that'll really make the universe shake. And Random take notice…'

Stratos keyed in the navigation codes and a planet came up on the screen.

'There,' he pointed his bloodied hands at the screen. The Samlores looked upon their doomed target.

'Fro.'

Jake and Anji, running against the tide of frightened patients and staff, made their way back to Random's bed to find their friend already trying to put his clothes on.

'Random!' said Anji breathlessly.

'I heard,' he replied.

'Sir, please you must reconsider!' pleaded Skateboard, 'You are not well enough to leave the Valetudinarium, let alone take on a genocidal maniac!'

'He's just destroyed an innocent planet, Skateboard. Billions of lives have just been lost,' said Random as he struggled with his shoe laces. 'Not only that but he said my name specifically. The people here will know who I am and will probably arrest me.'

'That won't happen,' said Jake. 'But what are we go-ing to do?'

'We have to follow him, whoever he is, and make sure he doesn't do it again.'

'Random, it's got to be a trap,' said Anji.

'Definitely, which is why as soon as we are back at the Venus II I'm dropping you all off on the first peaceful planet we pass.'

'No!' cried Anji.

'Definitely not!' exclaimed Jake.

'Sir, you have got to reconsider. We should work with the authorities to put a stop to this, I'm sure they will protect you...protect us!'

'But Skateboard, we have no idea why he even wants me. I have to know. Now, I want you to plug yourself into the mainframe and download my medical records. The nurse delivered my tablets before this all started, so as long as you know how to treat me, I can rest while we try to find this monster and think up a plan to stop him. Now do we have a deal?'

Skateboard sighed. What Random said about his anonymity being compromised rang true. They did need to get away, but he knew how ill his friend still was, and how long he needed to recuperate.

They also needed more information on this lunatic...and considering the weight of the genocide of the Osirons on the conscience of Random, now a whole planet had been blown away, somehow, in his name.

'Sir's right, Jake, Anji, we have to get him to the Venus II.'

'Right... I have an idea,' said Jake.

The Doctor was rightly shaken by the events of an hour ago. They all were. The tragedy of Fro's destruction had led to two different methods of instant reaction. One was of utter shock, grief and barely being able to comprehend what had just happened and the other was mad hysteria. The Doctor had wanted to do both simultaneously but instead, she shut down and sat in silence, totally shocked.

She had connections with Fro, very personal ones. Her parents had retired there. After a combined century of dedication to medicine, they were her heroes and now they were gone. She never even had a chance to tell them how much she loved them. Like so, so many.

So many arguments unhealed.

So many unsaid goodbyes.

She had wiped the tears from her eyes and was in
the middle of a sympathetic embrace from one of her duty nurses when she remembered the name that the terrorist gave was also the same name of her patient.

Random.

It was him, wasn't it? The boy whose body didn't make sense. The boy who should have been torn apart by the radiation he had consumed.

The boy who was lying in the East wing right now. She had to get to him.

She had to raise the alarm...but first, there were some questions she wanted to ask...

*

Racing to his bedside, she bolted down the endless corridors of the Valetudinarium, knocking still panicked beings out of the way as she screamed for space.

By the time she made it to the east wing, she knew that she was too late.

There was a mass underneath the badly made bed sheets but the patients belongings were nowhere to be seen. Neither were the bag of half gone off grapes that were plonked on the bedside cabinet.

Desperately, she whipped the bed clothes away, exposing nothing more than two pillows in the space that Random should have been occupying. Panting in anger, she tore away to the alarm button on the wall and plunged her slimy tentacle against it.

'Security alert, security alert, we have a sick patient missing from east wing bed 148!'

*

Somewhere else in the Valetudinarium, Random, who was hiding under a shroud on a gurney being pushed by Anji and Jake, stopped pretending he was dead and popped his head up from under the sheet.

'Bed 148. That's me!'

Jake, who had raided the utility cupboard after Skateboard had located it whilst downloading Random's data from the mainframe and taken two overgrown worker's overalls for himself and Anji, rolled up the sleeves of his arms that were far too big for him and gripped the gurney even tighter.

'Leg it!' he screamed.

6

ESCAPE AND RESCUE

By the time they arrived back at the Venus II, the hospital security team was waiting for them.

A line of six heavily armed officers, in baby blue uniforms that made them look like they were dressed in an armoured version of the scrubs the medical team were wearing, saw Anji and Jake wheel the gurney carrying the stricken Random and Skateboard into the hangar. As they cleared the entrance door, several other similarly dressed officers emerged from behind them and readied their standard issue batons.

'Random…' said Anji cautiously.

The Rodasian peeped his head from underneath his shroud and witnessed their predicament.

'Ah, right,' he muttered, unhelpfully.

'What are we going to do now?' hissed Jake.

'Skateboard! Use your knockout gas!' he cried. Nothing happened.

'Skateboard? Do it now!'

The AI robot poked his frame outside of the underneath of the gurney.

'I'm sorry, sir. I'm afraid I do not have a knockout gas stock built into my mainframe.'

Random rolled his eyes. 'Anything else?'

'You're coming with us,' said one of the security officers.

'No, we can't, you don't understand!' protested Anji.

'Listen to me, all of you!' cried Random, who was now sitting up and holding court as well as he could in his state. 'We know that this looks bad, but we had nothing to do with this.'

'Then why are you running?' said the officer.

'Because if we don't stop this lunatic then the entire universe could be in great danger!'

'But he asked for you, why would he do that?'

'We've travelled all over this universe, with the people we've saved we are bound to pick up an enemy somewhere along the line and look what's happened!' Anji interjected, 'He's got the power to destroy planets! He must be stopped!'

'That's something for the Space Seals to deal with, in the meantime we must place you under close surveillance,' said the officer, who started to move in with the rest of his men and women.

Anji and Jake began to back away towards the gurney.

'Seriously, us being here will mean nothing but danger, not just for you but for your patients! This psycho will clearly stoop to any level to find us. Please. You've got to let us go.'

'You are not going anywhere and that's final!' screamed the officer.

'Fine!' cried Random.

In that instant a piercing screech exploded from the tannoy system, rendering everyone incapacitated except Skateboard. He looked up at his friends, who just like the officers were crying out in agony as they held their hands over their ears. Gently, he pushed Anji onto Random's gurney, then Jake, and proceeded to fire up his rockets to hurtle them all out of the ambush and towards the Venus II.

Silently to everyone else but the little robot, the ship blipped like a car alarm as it's runway descended from its belly. In no time at all, Skateboard pushed them all up the runway and into the ship and using his wireless capabilities, instructed the ship to withdraw the runway and fire up the engines. As the officers tried to pick themselves back up and fight the horrendous noise away from their focus, the Venus II lifted up on its haunches and soared above them towards the security door that would see the travellers to freedom.

'No!' protested the officer, who try as he might, was so incapacitated by the noise that he was unable to radio into control to keep the doors closed. The Venus II sailed away towards its escape and as if by magic, the doors opened accordingly and before the officers could act, it was gone.

As soon as the Venus II disappeared from view, the high pitched noise died away. The security officers rolled around on the floor, wounded by their ordeal.

The officer who had confronted Random and his friends finally managed to use his radio.

Shaking, he whispered the words, 'Inform the Space Seals.' before finally losing consciousness.

Onboard the Venus II, Anji and Jake sat shaken on the sofas in the mid-section as Skateboard began to skuttle towards the cockpit.

'Jesus Christ! What the hell was that?' said Jake as he shook his head, the sound refusing to budge from his eardrums.

'I'm so sorry about that,' said Skateboard from the cockpit. 'I managed to hack the Valetudinarium's comm systems and incapacitate their security detail to give us time to escape.'

'You could have warned us!' bit Random, who was lying back on the gurney again, digging his fingers into his ear canals. Finally he had something else to add to the list of physical ailments he was currently experiencing.

'And give away my escape plan? Apologies, sir, but it was a spur of the moment thing.'

Anji shook her head. 'At least we got away. Now what?'

'Miss Anji, please take Random to the medi-bay,' asked Skateboard.

'No, Skateboard, we need to talk about what we are going to do next.'

'We will do so in the medi-bay, now hurry please.' Anji gave Random a sympathetic look and reluctantly, the red and blue boy allowed himself to be helped by his friend off the gurney. As his feet touched the ground they gave away a little. He was still pretty weak...in no state to rush head first into a war with a man with a vendetta against him.

As Skateboard initiated the Venus II's cloaking device, which hadn't been used in a while but thankfully still worked, the ship sailed silently, noticeably in the blackness of space once again, voyaging close towards the debris of what used to be the planet Fro, leaving the Valetudinarian far behind.

Stratos sat brooding in the Admiral's chair on the bridge of the Orbital. He had ordered his subjects to clear the freighter of the corpses of the dead, demanding that not one was missed and giving them an option to be creative in their disposal methods.

He'd done it. Besieged a battleship the likes the Space Seals couldn't afford to lose into enemy hands and destroyed a planet. It felt good. All of it. The destruction was like oxygen to his demented mind. And yet he was puzzled.

The distant hum of the Orbital's engines was disturbed by a knock on the bulkhead door.

Stratos grunted.

The bulkhead opened and the Commander swaggered in through the door and approached his Supreme Leader. He gave a bow.

'Commander.'

'Supreme Leader. We've finished disposing of the bodies.'

'Good.'

'It's not a pretty sight, you may want to use the wipers on the bridge view screens when we pass through them.'

Stratos ignored this visceral information.

'Tell me, Commander,' he croaked. 'Why that prison moon? Why not Earth?'

The Commander gave a nervous glance away from his brooding ruler.

'I don't understand, Supreme Leader.'

'When I was viciously apprehended by Captain Random I was about to destroy Earth. So tell me,' he pushed the chair's personal view screen towards his subject, 'How I happened to end up thirty million miles away?'

The Commander surveyed the digital readout on the monitor.

'Er…'

'Yes, that's what I thought. It isn't possible, is it? An escape pod has no warp capabilities. So how did I move? Why did I not end up on Earth?'

'Supreme Leader…' the Commander stuttered. 'I'm afraid that I am not the most learned when it comes to star mapping.'

'Did you not attend school?' asked Stratos.

'I'm a Samlore, Supreme Leader…I burnt it down on my first day.'

'A pity…you could have been so much more,' he spat. 'But this…is disturbing me.'

'Supreme Leader, we have successfully obtained the one of the most powerful battleships in the known cosmos. With your adjustments we can make whole systems bow to your might. Perhaps this puzzle can be completed after your universal conquest?'

'You're right, Commander,' Stratos said, pushing the monitor away. 'It's time we continued our breadcrumb trail.'

The Commander smiled a sinister grin.' What shall we destroy next?'

Stratos got up from his chair and made his way over to the long console bank.

He trailed his finger down an image of planets and rested his finger upon one.

'That one,' he smiled.

The Commander licked his lips.

'I'll tell the men to fire up the weapons.'

Stratos took his finger away and looked down on the next planet to face the horrific firepower of his fury.

'No,' he said. 'I have a better idea.'

From the relative comfort of his sickbed, Random sat cross legged as he sat and listened to his friends chatter.

'Could it be someone from Genocia? I mean, there's no way that the Government was ever going to be having us on their Christmas card list after what we did there,' said Jake.

'That's true. And there's no way that its Lon or the others. As we know the Flux went away with Strakonis, he wouldn't do a thing like that, would he?' asked Anji.

'Now there's a word I wish I'd heard the last of,' groaned Random. 'No, it's no-one we have met before, that's for certain,' he scratched his head, 'Could be a hit man, someone acting revenge?'

Another jolt sent them sprawling as another chunk of debris hit the Venus II's shields and set the occupants of the ship at unease.

'Skateboard, we really have got to get away from here. Every jolt is a reminder,' complained Random.

'Of what?' asked Skateboard.

'Of the billions of lives that have been lost in my name!' he snapped. Random threw himself back on the bed. 'This is a nightmare. Like I'm being punished for what I did to the Osirans. I try to prevent genocide and yet I end up causing it two times over. I won't let any of you tell me otherwise so don't even try.'

Jake bit his lip. Skateboard whirred towards his friend.

'Sir, just give it a little while longer. While we are silent, the Space Seals won't detect us. If we hide just a little longer in the rubble then we'll have the information we need and we can go.'

'What are you doing?' asked Anji.

'I'm using the Venus II's long range sensors to scan for the battle freighter's vapour trail. When the scanners detect it, we will be able to follow in its jet stream and catch up with whoever is in control of it.'

'Great! Face-to-face with a madman we know nothing about!' said Jake.

'And someone who knows a lot about us, or him to be more specific,' said Anji pointing to Random.

Random tugged at the irritating drips that were pumping medicine into his bloodstream.

'I need to be stronger,' he said to himself.

'Can we ask for the help of the Space Seals?' asked Jake.

'Negative, sir. The Orbital has been stolen from under their noses. She's one of theirs and what's more Random has been named an accessory to Fro's destruction and they are looking for us. There's no way that they will help us, especially when we know so little about what is going on.'

'Talk about being in the dark,' huffed Anji. She sat beside Random and put her hand on his arm. 'Random, we're not going to let you blame yourself for all of this. What's important is that we stop this guy from doing it again.'

Random sighed. 'You're right. We need to find light in the dark. Somehow. But it's going to be difficult with an ill Captain and a crew who are fugitives from the law. Then again, if anyone can do it, it's us,' he forced a smile across his face. 'Jake, what are my levels at?'

Jake got up and looked at the digital readouts that adorned the wall behind Random's sickbed.

'Hmmm…' he said thoughtfully, 'I'm fooling no-one, I ain't got a clue what any of this says!'

'Fine, Skateboard?' asked Random.
'One of your kidneys is still failing to function properly.'

'Which one?'
'Your fourth one.'

Anji and Jake were wide eyed with shock. 'Say what now?' asked Anji.

'And what about the rest of me?'
'The lumber puncture you had in your spine has cleared up the mess in your back but your ninth ventricle in your heart is a little erratic. Am diagnosing for a cause now.'

'Nine!?' spluttered Jake. 'Aren't you only supposed to have two?'

'The Captain's body has been artificially augmented beyond even the most conventional of Rodasian biological make-up,' said Skateboard. 'For sir to function the way he does he is required to have a more complicated set-up than most lifeforms in the galaxy'.

Anji eyed Random.
'Has he got more of everything?'
'Down girl!' said Random cheekily, making Anji blush.

'No wonder you're so fast with a heart that big,' said Jake.

'No wonder you feel so much loss,' said Anji. Random didn't acknowledge the remark. It wasn't just loss he felt, it was responsibility. To all in his care and to those who had perished on Fro.

'So, I'm still a bit of a mess, yes?' he asked.
'Statistically speaking, sir, you're running at 68% capacity.'

'That's not bad, just over half!'' said Jake.

'It's not good enough. How long until I am back to my old self, Skateboard?'

'There's no telling, sir. I hate to tell you this but there's no evidence to suggest that you will ever be back to normal. Your strength is way below what it was before the incident and although the drugs that the doctor prescribed will help you heal quicker, there's no telling what that radiation did to you in the long run.'

'Hang on, Skateboard, you're not telling me what I think you are telling me, are you?'

Skateboard's diodes sighed.

'Sir, we have to proceed with extreme caution. If you front up to this menace before you are well enough to do so, there's a very high chance that your body will descend further into radiation sickness. Overexertion could lead to cellular degeneration that would lead to irreparable damage.'

Anji and Jake felt tense and nervous.

'You mean he could die?' asked Anji.

'It's sadly possible, yes,' confirmed Skateboard. His circuitry was not built to cope with the emotion he was feeling in his artificial reality chip. He wasn't built to give bad news to people. He was built to move things and do odd jobs for masters. Skateboard was never meant to feel remorse or stress and worry. But now his fears were out in the open, he thought it would help him feel a little better. After seeing the faces of his humanoid friends, he realised just how wrong he was.

'But I hasten to add that this is an extreme worst case scenario. If you stay in bed and let your metabolism heal you then there's a chance that you shall continue to lead a life.'

'Just not the same as I had before, no?'

'No.'

'Skateboard, I can't do it, man,' Random said, his voice soft and understated. 'If I don't do anything there's a chance that more people will die. I can't let that happen. I was made to prevent things like this from happening and that is what I will do.'

Skateboard sighed and bowed a little.

'I understand, sir.'

'We're right behind you as always,' said Anji. Random smiled at her. 'You would be even if I asked you to keep out of danger, wouldn't you?'

'Anything for a friend!' said Jake, who gave Random a big bear hug. The Rodasian groaned a little, leading a sheepish apology from Jake.

A little alarm went off, breaking the moment for the travelers.

'What's that?' asked Anji.

'Security warning system,' replied Skateboard. 'The Space Seals have caught up with us.'

Outside in the vacuum of space, four by-jets scoured the vicinity for any activity. Light, slim and nimble, these one manned crafts were able to negoti-ate the huge boulders of rock that were travelling in their own dead slipstream, parts of what used to be the planet Fro flowed like rocks down a gentle woodland stream. Space was as silent as always. It was the calm well and truly after the storm.

Because of their actions in escaping the Valetudinarium, Random and the others were now fugitives in the sector and local traffic control had failed to notice a vessel of the Venus II's description leaving the general area. The local space was now awash with activity as the Space Seals not only began their investigation into the abduction of the Orbital but the destruction of Fro and the whereabouts of the Venus II.

Anji was perplexed as to how, with a cloaking device, the had been found.

'How?' she cried.
'They must have picked up on our own vapour trail,' said Skateboard. 'I'd better remember that in future situations.'

One of the by-jets barrel rolled past a massive rock and in doing so, missed the invisible Venus II's hull by a matter of centimetres. And yet, it failed to detect the ship even with such close proximity to it.

'Phew,' Jake blew out his cheeks. 'I don't think we can stay here much longer.'

The travellers, barring Random, had convened in the cockpit and witnessed the close shave. As the by-jet continued to spiral away, the alarm died down.

'Yeah! Have you picked up the vapour trail yet Skateboard?'

Skateboard ran a command through the systems.

'It's going to be difficult with all of this local interference to obtain it so quickly, I'm afraid.'

All of a sudden, there was ding from the cockpit command station.

'Oh,' said Skateboard surprised. 'I spoke too soon.' He observed the read out internally. 'Got it!'

'You know, we could just hand this information to the Space Seals and let them deal with it?' said Jake. 'Then they can arrest us! We can't do that!' cried Anji.

'But Random...what if...' said Jake.
'Don't say it,' she urged. 'Then it might not happen,' she smiled at her friend kindly. 'Remember what Random said, "the light in the dark." Let's find it together eh?'

'Sure thing, I'm all for positivity in a universe of chaos. Right Skateboard, let's do it!'

'Actually, sir, why don't you type in the co-ordinates. This can be a part of your training to pilot the Venus II in the absence of myself or Captain Random.'

Jake looked hesitant. 'Well, if you're sure.' He slid himself into the pilot's seat and with guidance from Skateboard, punched in the co-ordinates that would take them towards the danger that lay ahead.

'Remember to link the coordinates to the vapour trail too, sir,' said Skateboard. 'Let us follow them at a distance at first. It'll be good to give our Captain enough time to rest as possible.'

'Good shout, robot,' cried Jake. He punched in a few more commands and gripped the steering column tightly.

'Ready?' he said to his friends.
Anji gripped tightly onto the headrest of Jake's chair.

'Do it.'

And with that, Jake smiled a stupidly smug grin as for the first time he sent the Venus II into warp and in a blinding flash, they disappeared from the wreckage, far away from the Space Seals, far away from the devastation of Fro and into the danger that awaited them.

It took a couple of hours for them to follow the vapour trail through the warp tunnel that formed like a kaleidoscope of colour around them.

The gang always marveled when they were travelling faster than light. The shapes and colours that enveloped them were enough to put them in a trance and forget about their dangerous mission.

During the journey, in the medi-bay, Random began to stir in his sleep. He had thought it impossible for him to fall into a deep slumber with all that was rushing through his thoughts but with his body still as broken as it was, a two hour nap could be the difference between having enough energy to stop the monster who had destroyed a planet and losing his life to the tyrant.

But unsurprisingly, the sleep was not as restful as Random may have wished. It was when he slept that he occasionally could see the mysterious figures of the ghosts of long ago who had whispered into his mind so often since his birth.

And for the first time since the incident, there they were again.

In the dark recesses of his psyche, Random stood in the mist and saw the familiar outlines of the impossibly tall blue man and the short and red skinned lady. He opened his mouth to speak, but they beat him to it.

'You know what will happen if you confront this menace, don't you?' said the female.

Random took his time to respond. 'I know what's likely to happen, yeah.'

'Then your conscience is clear,' said the man. 'You know your role in the universe. The sacrifices you are yet to make?'

'I have a rough idea of what will happen there too,' he replied.

'Random, there is a force of terrible evil swarming through the cosmos, wiping out entire civilisations like a virus. You were created to bring hope and balance to Rodas. Now, the universe needs you more than even those who you are destined to save back home. But take heed, he thinks he knows you, but he doesn't. Not really. Not the person that you are now, anyway.'

'What?' Random said back to the female. 'How would you know that? Come to think of it, I still don't know how you can contact me from the past!'

'We are not,' the blue man interjected. 'You will learn someday.'

And with that, Random awoke, only slightly less confused than he had been when he fell asleep. But his mind was jolted somewhat by a knock at the door.

'Hey,' said Anji tentatively. 'Sorry to wake you up.' 'I'm not so sure that you did,' he replied and sat up in his bed. 'Are we there?'

Anji nodded. 'We are, yeah.'

Random exhaled deeply. 'Right then, let's-'

'Random,' Anji sat next to her stricken friend and spoke softly, 'Listen, we've...I don't know how to tell you this.'

Random looked blankly into Anji's eyes and saw the sadness inside of them.

'It's happened again.'

Jake and Skateboard looked out of the viewing screen of the cockpit, silent, unable to utter a single word. To their surprise, Random, his bed sheet hugging his shoulders, joined them, closely followed by Anji, to see with his own eyes what she had told him back in the medi-bay.

When he saw what his friends had all seen, he wished it had all been a bad dream.

Finally it was Skateboard who broke the silence.

'The Magari system. Seven planets...three moons.'

'All gone,' said Random in horror.

Stratos hadn't just had his way with one planet. He ended up destroying all of them.

'Scan for survivors,' demanded Random.

'Sir, the chances of anyone-'

'Just do it, Skateboard!' shouted Random. He immediately followed it up with a softer, 'Please.'

Skateboard made the command through his wireless connection with the ship.

'Horrible,' whispered Anji. 'All those planets. How can somebody do something like this!?'

'This isn't just revenge for this guy,' said Random. 'This is sport.'

Jake shuddered as he witnessed the stillness of space. 'It must have been over so quickly. Bits of Fro was still floating about. There's barely anything left this time.'

'Completely vapourised,' said Random.

A tiny light began to blip in and out of existence on the dashboard.

'Sir,' said Skateboard. Random leaned over Jake in the pilot's chair and he took a look at the read out displayed on the monitor.

'One survivor,' exclaimed Random.

He bolted out of the cockpit.

'Hold up, where do you think you're going?'

'Well I'm going to rescue them of course!'

'Random, you need to rest!' stressed Anji.

'Anj, we have the chance to save a life, I have to take that chance!'

'No, you don't, but I can,' said Jake.

'I can't allow it,' said Random.

'Oh, so Anji can fill up at a petrol station in space but when there's a chance to be a hero-'

'It's not about being a hero, Jake, it's dangerous, you'll be floating in an atmosphere littered with debris.'

'I don't care, I want to do it!'

Random sighed.

'Skateboard, get as close as you can to the survivor. Scan their life signs, give Jake as much time as he can take to get her back here safely.'

Random shot a look at Anji.

'You'd better stand by in case he needs help too.' As Anji and Jake prepared themselves, Random made for the cockpit and sat down in his pilot's chair.

'This is worse than anything we've ever faced, my friend,' he said to Skateboard, 'Now I can't even stop them from risking their lives again for me.'

'Like you said earlier, sir, there's no telling them,' said Skateboard.

Random sighed. 'Just promise me one thing. If they do get in trouble, don't you dare try and stop me in getting them back in here.'

Skateboard's circuits whirred and he went back to his business of steering the Venus II right into the heart of the rubble of the dead planet.

7

ALL DEAD, ALL DEAD

That brilliant explosion.

The blinding flash that had torn the planet Alfrajetti apart It had ripped open the very core of their world, split it into a million pieces, shredding countless countries to smithereens.

Obliterating a planet that had hung in space like a jewel in a crown.

And for Io, the last Alfrajetti in the universe, it had slaughtered her people.

She couldn't move for the shock, the lightning that burst through the very crust of their world, separating her from her family forever.

Oh god - my family.

An inner voice calmed her. *If she had survived, there was every chance they might have done too, right?*

The ray of hope shone in her mind as another quake shook all around. It had been doing that ever since she had regained consciousness, but when was that again, she wondered to herself? How long had she been floating about in space on a piece of rubble that used to be her home?

How much time left before her oxygen supply finally diminished and sacrificed her to the coldness of space.

No, she knew she was the only one now. Another voice began pouring thoughts in her head.

All the others were dead.
Her Mother, whose look of terror burned into her as the crash of the explosion happened all around them.

Her Father, who was in the house at the time, readying the meal of which she and her Mother were preparing for outside in their garden.

Her friends, she didn't have a chance to say sorry to after she'd cheated her classmates out of a chance for winning the Interstellar Trigonometry Competition.

Or to her parents for the message they received back at home of her actions and how they led to the school being disqualified.

There would never be a chance for forgiveness, for redemption.

All dead, all gone.

She sobbed uncontrollably as another quake shook her about the rocky plane. She'd lost them.

And no matter what she could do, they would never come back to her. Never would she be able to speak to them, tell them how much she loved them all.

Never would she even be able to hug them.
Then she remembered that light, that flash that interrupted her last, helpless look at her Mother and now here she was. Adrift. Alone.

It was slowly becoming harder to breathe.

Not long now, she thought to herself, not long before her lungs were on fire, gasping for air.

Not long until she would be with them again.
As she closed her eyes, she thought that she could see a ship close by. And a figure, who appeared to be tethered to it, edging closer and closer but still oh so far away. As yet another quake rumbled, and a portion of the ground near her disintegrated into nothingness, she wouldn't dare allow herself to hope that rescue was possible.

For her, it wasn't something that would redeem her for what she had done...

*

'I'm almost there!' cried Jake, who was starting to wonder whether he should have left the space walking to Anji in the first place. Trust him to want to play action man too. *No, concentrate, Jake,* he told himself, *concentrate on the survivor.*

It had been Random's idea to tether his friend to the Venus II, in the case of an emergency they could just wind him back into the ship. Skateboard was relieved that his Captain had made that decision as it meant that he could focus solely on piloting the Venus II around the huge rocks that were hurtling menacingly towards them. Even an expert would have had problems multi-tasking at a time like this and one such as he was having trouble keeping Jake away from the rubble also.

'You're doing brilliantly, Jake, just keep doing what you're doing,' said Random into the microphone on the dashboard. 'How's he looking to you, Anj?'

Anji was monitoring her friend's life signals on another instrument inside the cockpit they were sitting in.

'His heart rate is through the roof! Couldn't we have just beamed this person up?'

Random gave Anji a quizzical look.
'Beamed up?'
'Yeah. Surely you can do that with a ship like this.'
'Nobody can beam people up as you say, Anji.' She huffed. ' Well, I know some people who can.' 'Are they real?' asked Random.
'Well, no, but-'

'Well there you are then,' he replied. 'Jake, move 0.72 degrees to your left, do it!'

Jake punched in the commands into his wrist computer and yelled as he spun to the left, dodging a huge jagged piece of what used to be Alfrajetti.

'Woo! Thanks for the heads up! I'm almost there!'

'Jake for zarks sake, be careful! The infrastructure of the debris the survivor is floating on is starting to fall apart!'

'Oh great, any other good news you've got to tell me?' he replied sarcastically.

'Random says that there is no way we can beam you out of there,' said Anji.

'That's not helpful,' said Random.
'Yeah, I kind of gathered that when no-one said anything when I was volunteering for this, Anj, but thanks all the-'

The comm link died.
'Jake?'
Random flicked the communications switch again.
'Jake!'
'His life signs have stopped!' said Anji, her words anguished and worried.

Random punched in a few commands and an image of Jake flickered onto the scanner.

'The radiation from what is left of the planet Alfrajetti is interrupting our communication with him,' said Skateboard.

Random and Anji looked at one another.

'Nothing we can do for him now,' said Random as the Venus II lurched again missing another massive block of rubble. 'Come on mate, you can do it.'

'Hello? Hello?' Jake muttered but there was nothing but silence in reply.

'Oh no!' he looked back to see if the Venus II was still there and to double check that it hadn't smashed into what was left of a fairly big planet. He breathed a sigh of relief. There it was, dancing around the debris like an ice skater around rocks.

'Right, looks like it's all down to you now, Jakey,' he said to himself. He gulped.

As he moved in closer he could see the immobile form of the sole survivor of the terrible atrocity that Stratos had committed. Surveying their surroundings, Jake began to wonder how on earth they had survived. If they had!

No, Jake, he told himself, don't think like that. If his travels with Random hadn't only opened up his horizons to a universe of impossibilities, it had also taught him that there was always a chance.

So close now, Jake prepared the helmet that Random had dug out for him. It had a seal that locked to the person wearing it, so at least the survivor would be able to breathe, but the ravages of deep space would leave them susceptible to radiation without the whole body suit that Jake was wearing, so he'd have to act fast.

Io watched as the stranger tumbled closer and closer. As she supped what little air she had left, she turned her head and remembered.

No, her last memory wasn't of her Mother...it was that man. That thing. Grinning at her. Taunting her. Telling her to pass on a message…

'I got you!' said Jake triumphantly. He landed knee first and bent down in preparation to scoop the survivor up in his arms heroically like a knight in shining armour. Suddenly, another tremor erupted all around them and no sooner that Jake had put his arms underneath Io's semi-conscious frame, the ground beneath them completely gave way.

Jake screamed and gripped on to her tightly as he was showered with rubble and debris. He did his best to protect her but the devastation was such that she was already caked in it. He had no time to punch in the coordinates back to the Venus II, nor could he call his friends to wind them back in.

He had to do it.

With no time to do anything else, Jake, holding Io close to his chest, pressed the button on his side that activated the system to haul them back in.

With a horrendous jolt, both of them started to hurtle backwards towards the Venus II, slaloming around the flotsam and nasty looking rocks which were ping-ing around them like a pinball in an asteroid field. Jake held onto Io as tightly as he possibly could, knowing that a slip of his hand would undoubtedly send her hurtling off into space and all of this would have been for nothing. He cried out in terror, unable to see their path back, half not wanting to see it for fear that he would probably black out anyway.

The cord snaked around and around the asteroids reeling them both in like a fishing rod. Jake's eyes began to cry tears from how tightly he had screwed them shut.

And then suddenly, it was all over.
With a sharp crash on solid ground, Jake and Io skidded onto the metal floor of the Venus II.

'Anj, close the door, there's a draft!' shouted Random.

With a hiss, the ramp slammed shut. Jake, panting and disorientated struggled to get to his feet.

'There's no time to waste, get her in the medi-bay now,' cried Skateboard. Jake bent down, picked her up and proceeded to rush as fast as his wobbling legs would carry both of them.

Io took a sharp gasp for air and her eyes exploded open.

'It's okay, I've got you,' said Jake.
'You,' her voice was hoarse, it hurt her to talk. 'You should have left me out there.'

And with that, Io lost consciousness completely.

The crew of the Venus II spent the next couple of hours waiting patiently for Skateboard to run the de-contamination process in the medi-bay and making sure that it was safe for the others to enter.

Anji handed Jake and Random a cup of tea, the for-mer still in his spacesuit with his helmet propped on the sofa next to him. Random sat cross legged on the chair opposite and blew on his drink thoughtfully.

'I can't understand why she wouldn't want to be res-cued,' Jake said as he took the cup in his grasp.

'Nor can I, at the end of the day you'd have thought that she would be nothing else than grateful,' said Anji as she popped herself down next to him.

'Survivors guilt,' said Random. 'She's the last of her kind. Nobody in the universe would want a title like that.'

'She's seen her whole world burn,' said Jake, 'And for what?'

'Nothing,' said Anji, sipping her tea.

'Don't you wait for it to cool down first?' asked Jake.

'All that she has just seen. All that she has just lived through. No-one would ever get over that. No-one should have ever survived that,' Random stopped staring into the middle distance and focused his attention back onto his friends. 'Anji, Jake, I think we should be extremely cautious with how we proceed. There's an awful lot that isn't making sense here.'

'Like a man going about the galaxy destroying planets just to lure you into a trap?' said Anji.

'And not knowing anything about said bloke and why he is doing what he is doing?' continued Jake.

'And how a planet explodes and yet a life form is able to survive, not only that but live in the vacuum of space for a period of time,' concluded Random.

At that moment Skateboard rounded the corner and entered the mid-section.

'How is she?' asked Jake.

'She's stable. The contamination process has concluded its cycle so there is no risk of radiation exposure. I've given her an oxygen mask. She was out there for quite a while.'

'Do you know how long?' asked Random.

'It's hard to give a precise time but I estimate she was without oxygen for roughly thirty earth minutes.'

'Half an hour!' exclaimed Anji. 'That can't be right.'

'Like I said, miss, it was an estimation.'

'Has she come round?' asked Random.

'She has sir yes, but please, try not to distress her. She's been through a lot.'

'Skateboard, is it possible for her kind to be able to live in space for as long as that?' Random knelt down by his robot friend's side.

'It's difficult to say. The Alfrajetti's lung capacity is stronger than many humanoids, but to the best of my knowledge nothing could survive out there for as long as she did.'

Random sighed. 'Right then. We've been on the back foot since the start. We've had nothing but questions about this whole thing. Now it's time to get some answers.'

Io lay motionless, gazing up at the medi-bay ceiling, her oxygen mask planted protectively over her nose and mouth. Cotton sheets tucked her into place on a bed that sat next to one that looked like it had recently been used. Suddenly she heard footsteps approaching her. She shot a glance to the door and saw the half red/half blue figure of Random standing before her.

'You should have left me there,' she groaned.
'That's funny, normally someone would say, "thank you" if you'd just rescued them from death.'

'I've died already today.'
Random sat himself on the bed next to Io. 'What's your name?'
'Io Radousen.'
'Nice to meet you, Io Radousen. I'm Random.' Io stared blankly at him.
'You're nothing like I imagined you to be.'
'So you've heard of me then?'
'Briefly,' she shifted uneasily. 'Recently.'

'How come?'

Io closed her eyes. A single tear fell onto her cheek.

Feeling her pain, Random changed tact.

'You know I've not been well myself. I might never be well again. The last thing I should be doing right now is taking part in a wild goose chase around the galaxy. The worst part of what I am being led into isn't what is at the end of the journey, oh no, that part that really boils my blood is seeing nothing but total and utter devastation. All those lives that have been lost. All in my name. All in a madman's dream. Apparently this is all my fault. So I can forgive you for not wanting to talk to me right now, Io. I don't think I will ever find the words to express how truly sorry I am for all of this but I cannot put a stop to what is going on unless I know more of what, and who I am dealing with. So please, Io Radousen, help me.'

Io stayed silent, trying to sum up the words.

'You're right. I do hate you. I hate that the very mention of your name has brought me so much pain and anger. I hate that there are billions of souls out there lost thanks to what he has done, but I don't hate you as much as I hate him.'

Random moved closer to her.

'Who is he?'

Io broke down in tears. Random got up and picked up a box of tissues left on the side and handed them to her.

'Please,' he cooed, 'Take your time.'

Io didn't raise the tissues to her face. She held them tightly in her fist as she remembered what had happened to her.

'I don't know why I was chosen. I don't know why he picked on me. Believe me, I wish that he hadn't. But for some reason I was the one he wanted to use.

'My family and I were getting ready for a meal I had planned. I wanted to say sorry to them for the way I had been acting recently. My school,' she snorted, 'Not that it matters but I've not had the best of times there lately. So I wanted to make it up to them. To say sorry. I'd even gone to the trouble of paying for the food myself. It was just us. It's always been just us. That's why I felt like I needed to make a great effort to make things right with them. They don't...didn't have another child to fall back on when I got things wrong.

'Whilst we were readying out in the garden, I heard something strange, like a humming coming from the sky. As my Mother and I looked up, we saw this huge...ship, just hanging there in the sky.

'Before we could call for Father, what good that would have done, there was this strange light, like an explosion that burst from it and crashed down upon us. The last thing I saw of my world was my Mother. She was terrified. I was terrified.

'Then...' she broke off for a second, allowing herself to try and sob the memories out of her system. 'Then, all of a sudden we weren't on Alfrajetti at all. I was somewhere else. I was afraid and so I called out for my Mother and then for anyone who may be listening.

'Suddenly I heard heavy footsteps coming my way. The darkened room became light and,' she shuddered, 'I remember seeing him. I was too frightened to scream. I just stood there shaking, like a coward, as this... mon-ster approached me.

'He was…'
Io broke off again. Random put a reassuring hand on her shoulder. 'It's okay, take your time.'

Io choked back the tears and continued.

'He was made of metal. There wasn't much about him that was recognisable as anything I'd call Alfra-jetti. He was so tall, his arms and legs huge, powerful. His head was similar to ours, I suppose. But he spoke in a metallic voice, and his eyes... his eyes... were black.

'He told me that I was lucky, that I had been chosen, like it was some kind of competition. I said to him, "chosen for what?"

'He said, "chosen to watch."
'The next thing I know a couple of his hideous henchmen took my arms and pinned me up against the glass. I could see it all. My home, the moons of Alfrajetti, the entire system. And then I could feel a buzzing sensation underneath my feet. I tried to keep upright but his thugs did that for me. And then…' Io began to cry uncontrollably. 'I saw it happen. At first they hit

my world and I saw everything I have ever known burn up before my eyes. He killed them. He killed them all. And then he told me he enjoyed it so much that he'd do it to them all. They threw me to the floor, I pleaded with him but no matter how much I begged he chose not to hear me. And so it happened. One by one all of the planets burned.'

Random himself was moved to tears. He sat there in silence, listening to the horror of what had happened.

'They then picked me up, held me clean off the floor and held me close to his horrible face. I can still feel his cold grasp squeezing my cheeks as he told me to pass on a message. He said, "Tell Random to meet me at the Eye of Avalon. Tell him that I shall be waiting for him there and the killing does not stop until he is here, on this ship, ready to face his destiny." And then he told me that there was one other survivor. My Mother. He'd also taken my Mother.

'And he said that he wasn't going to release her until you were facing him and I had passed on the message.

'I begged him, I begged him to leave her alone but he threw me away, tossed me away like garbage, laughing at me as he did so. He said he'd do with my Mother whatever he liked. I begged him but it was like I was no longer there. I was just an insect to him. Something to be ignored, swatted away. The next thing I know his vile helpers held me up again and one of them forced something into my throat. I choked as I felt his slimy fingers push whatever it was deeper and told me to swallow it. And then... he told me his name, he told me he would be waiting for you and that you shouldn't keep him waiting too long or else more star systems would burn. He then said I wouldn't have long either and with that, I was torn away just as quickly as I was pulled from my home planet.

'Then something happened. I woke up and I was on a piece of harsh ground. I didn't recognise it but when I looked up I could see the starry night sky.

'The earth around me shook and buckled like an earthquake. I then realised where I was. He had abandoned me on the wreckage of my home. But I didn't scream. Although he wasn't there I could feel him watching me, laughing at my pathetic existence. I promised myself that I wouldn't scream again and that I should die where I was. I didn't want to continue liv-ing. Not even with my Mother safe. I wanted to believe that he had spared her too but I knew he hadn't done so out of kindness.

It was there that I left my life and embraced the thought of death. I still do.'

Random struggled to take it all in.

'Who is he? What's his name?' whispered Random. Io looked at Random square in the eye.

'Stratos.'

Random left the medi-bay and allowed Io to fall to sleep. Despite knowing how restless she was going to find it, she preferred it to not being awake.

His mind was racing.

Stratos. He had never heard that name before. How could it be that someone hated him so much and would destroy so many other lives just to get through to him, to display such utter barbarity on a scale that was inconceivable and that this person was not known to him?

Silently, he strolled down the corridor leading to the mid-section and finally the cockpit, haunted by Io's account of events. Haunted by what had happened.

Haunted by what he was going to have to do next. Anji, Jake and Skateboard had listened to every word. They had been monitoring the conversation from the cockpit on the surveillance system in the medi-bay, in place in case of a medical emergency. As Random walked slowly into the cockpit, he saw their sad faces. Anji and Jake both leaned in to give him a hug. He accepted it gratefully and buried his head on their shoulders. As they collected themselves, it was he who broke the silence.

'Skateboard, run a background check on Stratos. See if we have had any contact with him, no matter how directly or indirectly, we have got to find out how he knows about us.'

'Yes, sir,' said Skateboard.

'What are we going to do?' asked Anji. 'This Stratos guy, he's destroying whole galaxies. Just to get through to you.'

'I know,' Random slumped in the pilot's chair. 'He hates my guts and he is blowing planets apart just to make sure that I am listening.'

'What kind of a monster would do such a thing?' asked Jake to no one in particular.

'Possibly the greatest threat the universe has ever known,' said Random solemnly.

'Sir,' said Skateboard, 'I've concluded my background check on Stratos and there is nothing in the universal databanks regarding his existence.'

Random got up out of the chair to check the readouts himself.

'That's impossible.'

'I'm afraid it isn't, sir.'

'Check again.'

'I have done, sir, there is nothing on file concerning anyone of that name.'

'Maybe it's a code name?' said Jake.
'Maybe he's hacked in and destroyed his files?' asked Anji.

'I'm not so sure, it would take a genius to do that,' said Skateboard.

'We are talking about someone who can harness weapons together to kill off a planet, it isn't out of the question,' said Random.

'Perhaps not, but we have to accept all possibilities at the moment,' said Skateboard.

'Such as?' asked Random.

'Such, as, sir, that yes, there is a slight chance that Stratos could be a code name, or that he has hacked into the universal databanks, or that my theory is correct...'

'Would you like to share it with the class?' asked Random.

'That Stratos doesn't exist in this universe at all.'

8

FOR WHOM THE BELL TOLLS

Stratos had already inflicted more rage upon the universe than anyone had ever dared to comprehend. The ripples were being felt across the cosmos, news of the horrific atrocities he had carried out were becoming nightmares that haunted neighbouring star systems as they prepared their defences. Yet almost all the rulers of the planets who nervously anticipated the Orbital's arrival on their doorstep knew that there was nothing they could do to stop his wrath without considerable help from the intergalactic military, and Stratos knew that they would be pursuing him even as he smashed his fist repeatedly into the confines of the Admiral's quarters.

His rage had been peaked by something that had disturbed him greatly. Something that had plagued his mind ever since he regained his strength, his life, his overriding ambition to eliminate Random once and for all.

The truth.

It had stared him in the face ever since his ascension from near death to immortal.

There was nothing here in this cosmos he recognised. Sure, the star systems looked the same when he looked them up on the computer but there was so much that was different.

Worlds he had vanquished in the past still existed.

People he had murdered still lived.

Places he had known were missing.

His fingers had trembled when he requested information on his own home world of Draxo. It had been so long since he'd left, he'd given up so much for supremacy but it still felt like home to him.

And there were people who were so dear to him, torn away by his ambitions of power that as far as he knew, were still living on that pile of rubble that had promised so much but now stood on the brink of extinction.

He found the truth in his search...and it shredded what little compassion he still had in his cold metal heart.

Draxo didn't exist.

Draxo had never existed.

They were all gone...or had never been born at all, never colonised from the Earth.

Wherever he was...this wasn't home.

He was marooned.

He had let out a cry of pain and fury so loud the whole battle freighter had heard him.

But how? And then as he delved into the reason why he had ended up in a different part of space and a completely different universe to the one he knew and conquered, he discovered it.

The Eye of Avalon. That was what had brought him here. And when he'd marooned the girl he sought to manipulate to lure Random into his trap, he'd returned to his work and the answer to the question he so desperately needed to see was finally sitting there waiting for him.

All those calculations had led to this.

When he saw the answer, the formulae staring out at him from the computer screen, it pushed him past his limits.

The Commander stood outside the room quaking in his boots. He recoiled with every blow he heard, the savagery sound of metal being torn apart, ripped from the walls made his sweat cold.

He was welcome for the distraction of one of the Samlore foot soldiers approaching him.

'Commander, we have received confirmation on the long range scanners that a ship is approaching us.'

'The Space Seals?'

'No, Commander.'

He sighed. 'That is good news.'

Another bellow of fury exploded from within the quarters.

'You should tell him yourself.'

The foot soldier gave a whine of discomfort.

'Commander?'

'Well, go on, then.'

The foot soldier gulped hard and head butted his commanding officer hard in agreement, which did little to settle his nerves as he knocked tentatively on the door.

The banging stopped immediately.

'What!' barked the barely humanoid voice from within.

The foot soldier cleared his throat.

'Supreme Leader, we-'

The foot soldier never finished his sentence. In a split second a huge metal fist smashed through the door and splattered the him across the opposite wall.

As the Commander witnessed his bloody remains drip to the ground, he thanked his luck that it wasn't him who had interrupted the Supreme Leader's wrath.

Tentatively, he peeped through the hole that Stratos' fist had made and saw his Supreme Leader almost slumped against the view screen that gazed out onto the harsh blackness of space. The room was dark, save for the sparks and the small fires that had sprouted all around. All the furniture was splintered, the walls gutted, jagged tortured pieces of metal dangling down from the ceiling like daggers. A pipe had also been torn apart, flooding steam down upon Stratos' hulking frame.

'This better be good news Commander...' said Stratos, his voice chillingly calm.

The Commander rediscovered his composure.

'Supreme Leader...they are on their way.'

Stratos, his back to his loyal subject, grinned maniacally, his reflection staring back at the Commander through the hole in the door.

'At last.'

'So, what are you saying, Skateboard? And make it easy enough for Jake to understand,' said Anji in a vain effort to cut the tension within the mid-section.

'Hey!' said Jake before thinking to himself so hard that Anji could almost hear the cogs whirring within his brain. 'Actually, yeah, you'd better make it easy enough for me to understand.'

'I think I get what he's trying to say,' said Random, who placed a tray of drinking chocolate tenderly on the table that the gang surrounded in conference. They all took a cup except for Skateboard, leaving one for their guest who had insisted she would be well enough to discuss their next move with them. 'It's a parallel world, theory, right?'

'Indeed, sir,' said Skateboard to Random.
'Oh come on, that's way too sci-fi to even be a real thing!' said Jake.

'Really? After all we've seen and NOW you complain that things have gotten a little "sci-fi?"' said Anji, agog at her friend's reluctance to accept the idea.

'It is a pretty conclusive theory among many renowned scientists. In fact, it's a universal theory. That every decision you make sets you on another path,' said Skateboard, who although his diodes were not compatible with drinking chocolate, was doing his best not to be affronted by Random not even asking what he could get for him. 'For example, if we had decided not to return the engine part to the Osirans, Random would never have changed colour, creating an alternate timeline where the consequences of that inaction would have set a completely different future for us all.'

'Thanks for reminding me,' said Random, who returned to blowing on his drink to cool it down.

'Yeah, we might never have left that relaxation planet in the first place!' said Jake.

'Ugh, what I would give to be there now,' said Anji, who had been decidedly against the decision to give up their holiday in the first place.

'So somewhere out there, are an infinite number of us running around or sitting by a pool doing nothing?' said Random.

'Precisely,' continued Skateboard. 'And my theory is that Stratos is from a different universe to ours altogether. In his reality, you two are the worst of enemies but here a decision or action resulted in either Stratos not existing or something happened to him that stopped him from becoming a murdering scumbag.'

The gang looked in surprise at their little robot friend.

'I'm sorry,' he said sheepishly, 'Just trying to dust off areas of my language chip I barely use.'

'No, you're right, Skateboard, this man has destroyed billions of lives. He has the blood of a whole star system on his hands now...and he must be stopped,' said Random.

'Machine.'

A new voice joined them. it was Io, who was looking much better.

'Hey, how are you feeling?' asked Anji.

'I just saw my home planet explode before my eyes, my Mother could be being tortured by the machine who did it as we speak and I'm leading a group of strangers to their deaths.'

'You could have just said better,' replied Anji sharply.

'Io, pull up a pew and have some hot chocolate,' implored Random.

'I'd rather stand,' she replied.

'Well, I'd rather you didn't. You're still recuperating. You
did nearly die of asphyxiation you know and if I've learned
anything today it's to rest up,' Random pointed out.

Io tentatively took up a place beside Anji, who still
couldn't put her finger on why she had taken such a
dislike to the new arrival. After all she had been
through, she thought she may be a little more forgiving.
Yet despite her recent tragedy, Anji felt a sense of distrust
within her.

'I will do as you ask but my people are quick healers.
Well...physically speaking.'

'You said machine?' probed Jake.

'I did, and I see that as an accurate description,' she took up
the lonely cup and blew on the hot liquid.

'So not a man then?' said Random.

'He must have been once. Now he is more metal
than flesh.'

'Great, a psychotic cyborg then!' said Random.

'Yes. Are we going to confront him?'

'That's the plan,' said Anji.

'Just us four?'

'Actually, Skateboard's a pretty mean bad ass when
he wants to be,' glowed Jake, patting the AI robot on his
back.

'You do a great service in saying so, sir,' he clucked. 'Don't mention it. Maybe just don't go back to sounding like a space butler after I've said it, it dampens down the effect!'

Io ignored Jake. 'But I haven't told you where to find him. All he gave me was a message.'

Random leaned in towards her. 'Now sounds like a good time to hear it again.'

Io nodded. 'Stratos is waiting for you at the Eye of Avalon.'

'The Eye of Avalon?' asked Anji.

'Yes...erm…'

'Anji.'

'That's the rendezvous he gave me.' Io confirmed. She took a sip of her hot drink and replaced it on the table.

'Where's that when it's at home?' asked Jake. 'It's not somewhere that I am familiar with, I'm afraid, sir,' said Skateboard. 'But I'll consult the navigation system immediately.'

'Then as soon as we've found it, that's where we'll be going,' said Random determined.

'But it's a trap! It's so clearly a ploy to reel you in,' said Anji.

'My Mother is on that ship...if there is any chance that she may still be alive, I will do anything to get her back.'

'Oh, and that means setting us up?' said Anji.

'Anji!' replied Random. 'Io has been put in an impossible position. And we must do what we can to save her Mother and to save the universe from Stratos.'

'Can't we call for help?' asked Jake.

'I'm not sure the Space Seals will take our word that we are innocent in all of this,' said Anji. She shot a look of distrust at Io. Despite her tragic tale, Anji was concerned at how accepting Random was of her story. Yes, she had pointed out the obvious, but how could the five of them stop a man with the ability to destroy whole planets?

'Strength in numbers would be advisable,' said Skateboard.

Random placed his fore fingers on his lips in thought.

'Who else can we call upon? If we give away Stratos' location, supposed we drum up as many ships as we can, it could be full scale war. I'm not willing to do that. There should be as little opposition as possible.'

'So we're just going to go ourselves?' asked Jake.

'Yes.'

'With no back up plan?' asked Anji.

'I didn't say that, did I?' Random got up from his seat and paced around the mid-section. 'There's a chance that the Space Seals could already be on Stratos' trail. If that's the case, then we just have to make sure that we get there before they do. We would have to convince them we had nothing to do with events so far, however, and that would be a massive task in itself.'

'Sir,' came a voice from the cockpit.

Random, Anji, Jake and Io all got up and followed the voice.

'I have located the Eye of Avalon.'

'Where is it?' asked Anji. 'What is it?'

'I think this backs up my theory somewhat. The Eye of Avalon is a recent phenomena that was classified by astronomers on the edge of a prison star system known as the Flavorian system. It was identified as a reality fissure according to the universal data banks, which healed itself up and returned to its intended destination almost as soon as it appeared.'

'So it's a blip in space then?' asked Random.

'Yes, sir, it quickly healed itself and then returned to the actual place that Stratos had fallen through from his universe to ours. Call it an auto correction, as it were.'

'But what created it?' asked Anji.

'It's difficult to say without analysing it further. Best guess is that it's a sort of wormhole. It could have been pre-planned, perhaps your counterpart in the other universe intended to imprison him, sir,' said Skateboard to Random.

'I'd like to think another version of me wouldn't have so little disregard for others,' he said.

'Perhaps he intends to go back? Maybe he's figured it all out for himself. Maybe we don't have to go and follow him at all!' chirped Jake.

'You forget that Stratos has already callously wiped out entire civilisations to catch my attention. Would you really think he'd just pack up and go home now after going to all of that trouble? No, there must be another reason. We need to go now. Skateboard, where is the Eye of Avalon?' asked Random.

'On the cusp of SOL 3.'

'You're not narrowing this down for us, Skateboard,' replied Anji.

Random leaned over to inspect the read out.

'Oh,'

'Oh?' said Jake.

'SOL is your solar system and the 3 is...Earth.' Anji and Jake turned in horror to one another.

'Earth? Stratos is going to destroy Earth!' Anji cried.

'Not if we can help it! Skateboard, how long until we reach the solar system?' asked Random.

'Approximately 92 clicks,' came the reply.

'What are we waiting for?' said Anji. 'Let's go!'

Random hurled himself into the pilot's chair, pushed some buttons and forced a lever down and with that, the Venus II tore away and was thrown into lightspeed, leaving nothing in its wake as it shot off towards Earth.

As the brilliant colours of the lights peed tunnel whirled all around them Anji took Random by the arm.

'We can't let Earth be destroyed...' tears began to flow from her eyes, '...we just can't!'

'We won't' said Random, who got up and put a re-assuring arm around her and Jake. 'No more chaos. No more death. This ends with us.'

Io allowed herself to be swallowed by the shadows. She was sending these brave strangers to their deaths...

*

Stratos marched onto the bridge of the Orbital, its banks of instruments manned unconvincingly by a group of Samlores who had heard the powerful hy-draulics of their Supreme Leader's legs long before his brutal frame stood before them. All of a sudden they all decided, almost telepathically, to look busy.

'Report!'

'The ship is nearly here, Supreme Leader,' said one of the Samlores.

'Shall I power up the weapons?' asked the Commander.

'You would deprive me the pleasure of killing him with my own hands?' spat Stratos. 'Don't you dare sug-gest such a thing again.'

'Coming up on the viewer screen now, Supreme
Leader,' said the Samlore sitting at the scanner bank.
'On screen!'
The huge image of space shot up above them and nothing
else. For a few minutes, they all looked for signs of a
ship approaching until naturally it was Stratos with his
bionic vision who spotted it first.
'There!' he pointed. 'Increase magnification in quadrant
zeta four!'
The Samlore did as he was instructed. A slightly
larger spec of silver came into view.
'Magnify 200 percent,' Stratos instructed.
The image zoomed even closer.
'There she is!' exclaimed Stratos. 'There she is!'
'It's not a vessel that I recognise,' said the Comman-
der.
'You wouldn't,' said Stratos, his eyes transfixed on it.
'It looks in better condition than the last time I saw it.'
The sleek, streamline spacecraft shone and twinkled
on the viewing screen.
'The Venus II,' said Stratos in almost a whisper.
'It's heavily armed...and has a cloaking device which is
currently active!' exclaimed a Samlore.

'Then how are we seeing it?' asked the Commander.
'This is the Space Seals most powerful battle
freighter. It wouldn't let something as cowardly as a
cloaking device deceive it. How far away are they now?'

'14 clicks, Supreme Leader.'

'And it cannot see us just yet, no?'

'No, Supreme Leader. Due to our location we are obscured from both they and the planet below this moon.'

Stratos grinned. 'Good.'

He walked closer towards the screen. A alarm bell rang, alerting the Samlores to action stations.

'Oh Captain Random...for whom the bell tolls…'

*

The Venus II left light speed several hundred miles away from Mars to give its crew adequate cover if needed.

'Mars!' exclaimed Jake. He and Anji breathed a collective sigh of relief.

'So they haven't destroyed anything?'

'Negative, miss,' said Skateboard, 'The solar system is just as you left it.'

'It feels good to be back!' sighed Jake.

'We've got a lot to do to make sure it stays this way,' said Random. 'Skateboard, see if you can locate Stratos' ship.'

'Shouldn't be an issue, sir.'

'Won't it be difficult to locate with all the local traffic?' asked Io.

'What local traffic?' said Anji. 'There won't be any other spaceships around here. Well...a few satellites...'

Io tutted. 'What a primitive place you come from.' 'Oi!' said Jake, 'It may be primitive but at least it's still here.'

Io scowled at him.

'I'm sorry, that was quite mean, wasn't it?'

'Jake...remind me when I'm having a personal crisis again to not go to you about it,' said Random.

Jake felt his cheeks flood with hot shame. 'Sorry again, Io.'

'Stratos should be here...why isn't he here?' she said, ignoring Jake's apology.

'Don't be afraid, Io, you're safe here,' Skateboard re-assured her.

'If you had met the monster like I have...you'd never feel safe.'

'Any updates, Skateboard?'

'No, sir. There is no sign of Stratos' ship anywhere.' 'I don't like this,' said Anji.

'Could he be cloaked like us?' asked Jake.

'It's a possibility,' said Random. 'He's here some-where...'

'Sir!' exclaimed Skateboard. 'Incoming!'

Random looked up and from the cockpit window saw a bolt of energy fizzing towards them through the whirls of space.

'Evasive maneuvers!' said Random, as he picked up the Venus II's port wing. The spaceship shuddered as the volley of fire burnt right underneath it and continued to hurtle past them.

'No damage,' reported Random.

'A warning shot,' confirmed Skateboard.

'Can you get a fix on where it came from?' asked Anji.

The crew's breathing became collectively a little heavier.

'Already confirmed, miss,' said Skateboard. Random read the read out and pointed into the far distance.

'What? The moon fired at us?' said Jake.

'It came from behind the moon,' confirmed Skateboard.

'The dark side of the moon,' said Anji.
'There appears to be quite a build-up of background radiation obscuring it from our instruments.'

'Do we go and meet them head on?' asked Anji.

'No, we need to hang back, we can't be tempted any further,' said Random, 'for now at least.'

All of a sudden, the communications system cracked into life and a sinister, malicious voice bled over the airwaves.

'Do I have your attention...Captain Random?...'

9

THE ORDEAL

'Stratos,' Random said with utter contempt.

The malevolent, almost robotic tones shook the cockpit of the Venus II. Anji squeezed Jake's arm. He gave her a look of utter dread.

'Your voice is different and yet...it remains as arrogant and foolish as it always was to me.'

Random's frown fixed itself on his brow.

'How come you know so much about me? Because I've never even heard of you!'

'I have many an advantage on you, Captain. The odds are overwhelmingly stacked in my favour. You may think that you are safe, cowering like rats in your little tin ship, hiding from my sight. But I've always been able to get through to you someway, somehow.'

'You unspeakable abomination!' shouted Random, whose anger was rich for all to see. 'And you think de-

stroying whole star systems is a justifiable way of trying
to get through to me!?'

'Well…' said Stratos calmly, 'it worked, didn't it?'

Random's blue/red eyes began to burn intensely. 'And
now I have you where I want you…well, almost…' the voice continued.

Suddenly a bright green light began to shine around the
cockpit.

'What's happening?' cried Anji. She let go of Jake
and moved away from the light which had begun to envelop
Random.

'Stay away!' ordered Random but it was too late.

The beam reached out like a claw and trapped Io too
and due to his close proximity, Jake had also been caught
up in its grasp. As the brilliant light shone brighter
still, the figures of Random, Io and Jake disappeared
altogether. Anji had fallen against the dashboard, shielding
her eyes from the light and as it ebbed away, she put her
arm by her side and gazed in horror at the empty cockpit.

'Skateboard?' she muttered.

The robot had also been left behind. He checked
the computer. 'They have been taken…'

The next thing they knew, Random, Jake and Io were no
longer in the relative safety of the Venus II. The green
light dissipated and the trio were left alone in a strange
place.

'Where are we?' asked Jake.

'Oh no!' cried Io, who began to back up with extreme caution.

'We're on the Orbital…' said Random, '…he must have found a way to get past our shields.'

'How?' asked Jake.

Random took a look around and observed his surroundings. It looked as though they had materialised in a cargo bay, its grey decor yawning off the walls around them.

'The man can destroy planets, a little abduction clearly isn't past his capabilities either,' said Random, who noticed Io receding in the vast room. 'Io! Don't worry, you're safe,' he tried to reassure her.

'We are far from safe!' she screamed. At that moment the bulkhead door hissed open. A gaggle of Samlores marched into the room, armed with Space Seal issued laser rifles. There was nowhere for Random and his friends to run. Jake was repulsed by the Samlores salivating tusks, the hideous creatures clearly salivating at the prospect of torturing their victims.

The boy lifted his hands above his head. Random refused to offer them the gesture of surrender.

'You'll do my friends no harm otherwise you're get-ting nothing from me!'

The Commander leveled his gun squarely at Random's head.

'Come.'

*

Anji was pacing up and down, unable to relax. She'd just seen her best friends abducted by a madman before her eyes. Her mind was playing havoc with her anxiety.

'But they are going to kill them!' shouted Anji. Skateboard, despite his emotional limitations as a robot, was also feeling anxious at the prospect of what their friends could possibly be enduring right now as they were doing nothing but fretting.

'Please, Anji.'

He dropped the usual "miss" that he usually designated to her, hoping that addressing Anji by her actual name might actually help to calm her down. 'Hypothesising about the possibilities will not help them or us.'

'Well, what then?!'

'We need to take action…'

'Can we beam them back?'

'Negative, miss, we do not have that kind of technology on board.'

'You mean to say that we can replicate food and stop the need to go to the toilet but we can't beam about the place?'

'Yes, it's hard to conceive when you put it like that, but even if we could, I doubt that we could penetrate the Orbital's shields like they did ours…'

Skateboard left his sentence hanging in the air as his diodes began to whir, trying to form some kind of a plan in his main frame.

Anji sat on a chair, her left leg jiggling and proceeded to bite her nails, staring into space. She was sure that Random could handle himself. She'd seen it all before with him, even if the Rodasian was still recovering from a massive dose of radiation poisoning that had scrambled his body, but Jake...poor Jake. Why did he have to get taken with them? Why couldn't it have been her. If she could guarantee her friends' safety over hers, she'd sacrifice herself in an instant. And yet now she was stranded without them, again!Just like on Genocia.

Then she had an idea.

'I've got it!'

'Yes, miss?'

'We call the Space Seals!'

Skateboard's diodes moaned. 'Unfortunately my CPU has already calculated 2,793 possible plans of action and enlisting the help of the Space Seals didn't make it past the "bad idea" stage of elimination, miss.'

Anji got off her stall and knelt down beside her AI friend.

'Think about it. They are already looking for Stratos AND for us. If we can tell them we have nothing to do with all of this then we can get them onside!'

'Presuming, miss, that they believe us,' said Skateboard.

'We tell them the truth then, we have nothing to hide...come on! If you continue on your parallel world theory while we fly to them, we'll have even more evidence to back us up!'

A beeping alarm went off in the cockpit. The pair rushed into the small room.

'What now?' Anji complained.

On the cockpit view screen a large battleship loomed before them. Then another. And another.

And another.

Huge vast vessels, armed to the teeth with turrets and missiles, engulfed the tiny space that the Venus II was parked in. Anji gasped audibly at the sight of them, five by now. They looked a little like massive aircraft carriers in space, with smaller ships balanced on top of them. The battleship at the front was now so vast, so magnificent, Anji was terrified they were going to crash into them.

'It appears,' said Skateboard to his human friend, 'they've already found us.'

Random allowed himself to be manhandled roughly by the gang of vicious Samlores who clawed at his flesh as he was pulled and pushed towards what he assumed was the bridge. Between the shoving and the horrific feeling of his captors long nails scratching his skin as they continued their short journey from the detention cells, Random thought of Anji and Skateboard and how he hoped and prayed that they would not be stupid enough to mount an attack on the Orbital.

Not yet, at least.
With Jake and Io imprisoned behind a translucent shield, and both he and his friends manacled to make any chance of escape even less likely, he thought of all the chaos he could wreak given the chance.

He could easily tear the manacles apart, radiation poisoning or no radiation poisoning, he was sure that he still possessed the strength to decorate the blank corridors of the battle freighter with whatever made the Samlores the slimy weaklings he was sure they really were.

But for what?
No advantage. Nowhere to run. And so he was left with the inevitable.

Random had to face his enemy.

They came to a bulkhead door that hissed upward into the ceiling upon approach.

Random stared into the bridge of the ship. It's huge, multi leveled structure until recently was a hive of activity of people protecting the lives of countless species across the cosmos. Now, the monstrosity who stood imperiously before him dominated even the biggest of control rooms. For the first time, Random clapped eyes on a man who hated him more than anyone in the entire universe.

'Leave us,' growled the metallic voice. The Samlores obeyed their order and untidily filed out of the bridge back through the bulkhead door, which slammed shut behind them. Random didn't turn once from his enemy, not one second was lost.

He was never going to let him see fear...because there was none to feel.

The only emotion Random felt was rage.
'You look very different to how I last saw you,' whispered Stratos, looking out of the bridge into the vast blanket of space.

'Oh yeah, when was that then?' said Random snarkily.

'You were older. Much older. And purple. If my suspicions hadn't been aroused before our meeting then they would all be confirmed to me now.'

'Older? How? Who are you?'

'I am Stratos. And you are Captain Random.'

'I know who I am, thanks all the same!'

'A boy who was too scared to face the responsibility of saving his own planet that he ran across the stars, searching for a distraction, anything that would help him sleep at night...even if it meant the destruction of others.'
'Hypocrite!' cried Random, trying his best not to rise to the bait. 'You've destroyed countless lives just

to get my attention and here you are claiming that I am a killer when you have the blood of star systems on your hands!'

'One day,' continued Stratos, 'that little boy realised the power he possessed and what he could do with it and it was on that day that the universe fell into darkness. You see, Captain, that the Random I know and despise had been boiling away entire galaxies long before I encountered him. And that Random is very much a part of you too.'

'Lies!' Random spat.

'No,' Stratos moved in the shadows and proceeded to punch some instructions into a computer. A hologram of a star map, showing what Random presumed was the universe projected out of an unseen lens and swamped the space that divided them.

'Your universe…' said Stratos before punching in more instructions. Suddenly, several of the nebulas and star systems flickered and disappeared from view.

'Mine.'

Random gazed at the map, his breathing began to fall deeper. There were now gaping holes where twinkling stars used to be.

Stratos stayed in the background, circling his captive like a lion stalks his prey, ready to pounce, but he wanted to make this poor imitation of his best enemy squirm. Make him truly suffer for his other selves crimes against the universe. For whatever atrocities

Stratos had committed in this universe, they paled in comparison to those of the Random he knew and despised.

'Oh you saw to it that they all went. Tatmaria. The Dools of Mareen. Even the Kibarium cluster. All gone, destroyed, turned to nothing but dust. Even Spectronia.'

Random's eyes widened. 'Say that again?'

'That was where the power overwhelmed you, where you became the destroyer of worlds. Until then your lust for destruction was simply palatable to a rival like me but after that, you were simply unstoppable, you and your human friends. And when I realised that their home world was also the same that had left my people to die, it didn't take a split second to make me want to burn the Earth too.'

'The Flux,' Random said under his breath. His skin crawled. Sweat began to pour from his brow and his hands became clammy with terror.

So he had done it. Somewhere out there, there was a version of him who had used the Zedron Flux, just like he did, and allowed its power to consume and distort him. The thought that there had been a version of him in another universe who had made the same de-cision as he, to use the Flux to stop the Osirans, but then proceeded to committing incredible acts of genocide afterwards, sickened every fiber of his being.

'Little did I know that you were going to be there. You ambushed my armada before I had a chance to destroy the Earth and obliterated my plans. but putting an end to my revenge wasn't enough for you. You showed no mercy. Not even a little. As my men lost their lives all around me and my ship disintegrated under the might of your war weapon, I watched as you laughed at my pleads of mercy.

'And in that moment, you killed what little good may have ever been alive in me.'

'Stratos, this is insane,' said Random as he paced towards his enemy with intent. 'You're taking a horrific vengeance with me that does not exist in this universe, on the lives of innocents on a scale that is terrifying. The revenge that you are wreaking is not in this universe, I am not the Random you think I am.'

'No, but I know what you could become. Besides, you are forgetting. Although I realised that I had fallen sideways in space to another dimension, I still decimated this universe. My desire for revenge is dwarfed by my hatred for you.

'I cannot go home. I can never get back to my universe. The rift in space time will not allow it. So why shouldn't I transfer my power of destruction to this universe instead? I'll tell you why,' he pushed his face right into that of Random's. The red/blue boy saw the hideous biomechanical implants protruding through his flesh, his veins blue and puckered, his eyes as black as the heart of death itself.

'Because I can,' he snarled.

'Stratos,' said Random calmly, trying to regain his composure, still meeting the gaze of his enemy hard, 'The killing must stop now. It goes no further than here.'

Stratos emitted a blood curdling laugh, like a rusty chainsaw revving up in an echo chamber.

'Why? Who is there to stop me?' he cackled again, 'You?'

In a split second, Stratos' mighty claws had clamped around Random's arms and the boy was crashing against one of the walls. Random felt the sharp fragments of buckled metal dig themselves in his back and before he had any time to react, he was flying across the room before he landed in a heap, his head hitting the control bank hard at the opposite end of the bridge.

He coughed, a tinge of copper washing his taste buds. He tried to pick himself up but he was still too weak.

Not ready, not ready at all, he thought to himself as he began to black out, the final image he saw as he fought back unconsciousness was that of Stratos hurtling towards him, the floor shaking as he landed just inches from Random's stricken frame.

Random's tormentor knelt down in front of his prisoner and laughed.

'Evidently not.'

And with that, Random's eyes closed and everything went black.

Skateboard hated being lectured. An AI robot with the intelligence he possessed, talked down to at a rate of condescension that was off the scale? It was so embarrassing. Especially when the woman in authority who was talking to him and Anji was telling him nothing he didn't know already.

They had been forced out of the Venus II at gunpoint and escorted to the bridge of the massive battle freighter and forced to endure a dressing down of epic proportions by the Admiral of the ship.

Admiral Bagari was an impatient, no-nonsense woman at the best of times. This was not one of them.

'What's more,' she continued, as Skateboard noticed she seemed to have more stripes pinned to her tunic than there are on the American flag, 'Without full jurisdiction from the Space Seals you are nothing more than space vigilantes. I should have you both locked up for running away!'

Skateboard acknowledged the rank displayed on her tunic and thought it was best he stop her there, exactly eleven minutes forty-nine seconds after she started speaking. From the very moment they had strolled into the bridge of the battle freighter after the Venus II was brought on board, as a matter of fact.

'Admiral,' he said politely.

'Don't interrupt me, I haven't finished!' she barked. 'We have the Orbital in visual range, Ma'am,' said one of the exotic looking soldiers that sat, working away at their post. When Anji's mind started to wander, roughly three minutes into the Admiral's tirade about how they should both be arrested for harbouring a suspect, she'd been taking in her surroundings and admiring the vast array of alien beings who were working together. The officer who alerted the Admiral reminded Anji of a cross between a parrot and an octopus, an image she had never concocted before and probably never would again.

The Admiral strode away from Skateboard and Anji, who both made to follow her but were forced to stay exactly where they were by the dozen or so Space Seals who were leveling their rifles right at them.

'Magnify,' ordered the Admiral.

The Parropus did as he was told. A vision of the Orbital flooded the huge viewing screen.

'How far away are we?' she asked.

'Three hours, Ma'am.'

'Can't we just beam there?' Anji interjected.

'No we cannot just "beam" there. Their shield will be at maximum. Plus we don't want to startle the threat before we know precisely what they want to do.'

'That, Admiral, is what I've been trying to tell you,' said Skateboard. 'Now, please, listen to me. the Orbital has been hijacked by a criminal from another universe, who seems hell bent on revenge against our friend for a rivalry they possess in his reality. Stratos was destroying those planets to lead us here for one reason alone, the total destruction of Random.'

'Listen, robot, your story would sound more believable if you dropped this whole charade. If there had ever been a being as powerful as you say he is we would have known about him long ago, let alone this whole parallel universe delusion you seem to think magically explains this whole thing.' A prominent vein began to pulsate near Bagari's temple.

'But that's exactly the point, Admiral,' Anji interrupted, 'You don't know about him because he doesn't exist in this universe, that's what Skateboard is trying to tell you!'

'Then explain this to me,' she said through gritted teeth, patience busting at the seams, 'Where did this "Stratos" of yours pop up from? Huh? People don't just come into existence like that!'

'Err...Ma'am,' said another officer, this one looking more like a jellyfish in a uniform.

'What!'

'We've picked something else up on the long range scan.'

'Well go on then, what is it?'

'I...don't know,' stuttered the officer.

The Admiral marched over to the bank, her legs pumping with anger.

'We've got to convince her of our story!' said Anji quietly.

'I have a feeling she won't need much more convincing,' said Skateboard smugly.

He was right.

On the other side of the solar system to them, sitting between the Earth and Venus was something that no one in the history of the galaxy had ever seen before. The stuff of legend, the kind of thing little boys and girls write about when they want to grow up and become science fiction writers.

'What on Sevestia...' exclaimed the Admiral. There, for all to see on the long rang scan, was a

large swirling fissure in space.

Random awoke from his nightmare with a horrendous splitting headache. Upon braving the harsh white light that shone in his face, he soon wished that he hadn't woken up at all.

He felt his arms and legs being pulled apart, heavy iron bonds lashed around his ankles and wrists, hoisted up in the air like meat in a butchers shop.

'How kind of you to join us again, Captain,' beamed Stratos. 'I thought I'd invite your friends to join us. I wouldn't have been much of a host if I left them in their cell now would I?'

Random did his best to break free of his bonds, but it was no use.

'Don't you dare hurt them!' cried Random.

'Random!'

It was the familiar voice of Jake. Random's heart sank. He sounded terrified.

'Jake! Don't worry, it's going to be alright! Where are you? This light...I can't see anything!'

'He's not in a very comfortable position, Random,' chuckled Stratos. 'You wouldn't be either if you were pinned to something as uncomfortable as he is.'

'Random, please,' came another voice. It was Io.

'Oh, yes, she's still here too, my bait,' Stratos hissed.

Jake and Io were fixed with magnetic bonds to two identical slabs. Their heads were encased in what looked like hard hats to Jake. He tried his best to act calm but considering the Samlores that circled them and the horrific sight of Random being hung high in the air with a blazing light shone in his face, he feared the worst.

He knew that before the incident with the Zedron Flux, Random would bust them out of this no problems. He would break out of his bonds like they were paper and send Stratos' big metal bottom back into his own universe with one swift drop kick.

But Random was weak, injured. Defenseless.

And now for all the hope in the universe Jake was starting to lose faith that they would ever get out of this alive.

'Do you know what these are, Captain? No of course not, you can't see them, can you. Well let's just say that the Space Seals have a rather unethical way of dealing with prisoners from time to time. From what I can make out from the instruments, these helmets send pulses into the brain to make the poor tortured souls wearing them submit the truth. Well, I doubt there is any information these two can give me that would be handy so why don't we play a little party game?'

Random tried his best to keep pulling at his manacles, but every time he did he was zapped by an electrical bolt that seemed to come from nowhere.

'Oh, don't think I wasn't going to include you in this game,' said Stratos. 'Every time you yelp for mercy, or cry out in pain, another bolt surges through your bodies. Every time you bargain for your lives, the voltage will go up. Within minutes you'll all be too weak to put up any form of resistance but don't worry about that because the effects aren't long lasting...so we get to do it again. And again. And again! Are you ready? Let's play!'

It was the surge of lightning and the screams of Jake and Io that Random heard first before his own body was riddled with an indescribable searing heat.

'Stratos!'

'No, no, Random, you know the rules, don't go breaking them already now!'

'Please!' cried out Io.

'Oh dear, it looks as though the urchin from Alfragetti is the first to lose a point,' he turned to the Samlore who controlled the voltage on the torture instrument. 'You know what to do!'

The screams echoed around the chamber, as did the crackling energy of the electrodes that were boiling their way into Random and his friends.

'I think I have a name for my new game!' Stratos cried as he did little to hide in vain the pure enjoyment he was getting from seeing his enemies writhe in agony.

'No mercy...'

10

FOR ALL THE STARS IN OUR GALAXIES

Admiral Bagari was cross.

She paced up and down her bridge, arms behind her back, scowling at the two intruders who had so skillfully talked their way out of a prison sentence for accessory in galactic genocide. Not only were their powers of reason so on point and their words rang so true, but they'd also somehow managed to coax her last name out of her, so not only would she have to put up with them showing her up in front of her crew, who had spent the last three years hiding behind corners from her whenever she was on deck patrol, but now they saw her as an agreeable person.

She groaned.
Loudly.

'I thought you said you knew all about spatial anomalies?' she growled at Skateboard, who had positioned himself precariously balanced upon one of the command chairs.

'I do, Admiral, but not about this one.'

'So you tricked me?'

'Not tricked, Admiral,' cried Anji, 'He'll know soon.'

'Thank you Miss Gummadi,' he said in his usual polite manner. 'This is indeed fascinating. It appears that this anomaly is indeed a gateway into another dimension. Call it the Beta universe to our Alpha.'

'Why?' asked Admiral Bagari.
'Well, because we knew about ours first,' he said smugly.

'Alright, Skateboard, what are you getting at?' asked Anji.

'According to my calculations, the anomaly is a one way gateway into our universe. Caused by a cataclysmic explosion that had the ability to rip a hole through space/time. This is how Stratos managed to end up in our universe.'

'Then we are lucky he didn't blow up the Earth when he arrived!' said Anji.

'Negative, miss. The anomaly originally materialised in the opposite end of the galaxy, before snapping back here. Hence, why Stratos was able to snatch the Orbital.'

'Killing all of our people in the process,' Admiral Bagari interrupted. 'We got there first. No ship, no Stratos. Just hundreds of bodies, scattered around the quadrant, suffocated. Some of them we knew, we graduated with. Gone now. One day I might be able to cope with the responsibility of telling their loved ones.'

'That's horrible!' said Anji, her mind flicking straight back to what kind of hell Jake and Random must be facing as they spoke.

'That was nothing compared to what we saw next. As we followed the vapour trail we came across more and more death. Too late every single time. Continuously playing catch up. Too slow to save them. The universe will mourn the worlds that have perished. Just as soon as our armada has put an end to him once and for all.'

'Not without rescuing our friends first,' said Anji stoically.

Bagari sighed. 'We've a job to do. To protect the lives of billions of people. If I have the opportunity to blast the Orbital out of the sky before Stratos kills again then I will take it.'

'Then let us go and save them before you do!'
'Anji, no.'
'Why not Skateboard!?'
'You're leaning on the navigation port.'

Anji looked down and noticed that she had knocked the coordinates out of alignment when she forced her hands down on the control unit.

'We'll discuss that in a moment,' said Skateboard. 'First of all, we need to work out a plan to stop Stratos.'

Anji bit her lip.

'I'll have to call a conference meeting with the Admirals of our fleet. There's too much that could go wrong here and I alone am not able to make a definitive decision on what we do next, no matter what I say.'

'Fine,' she murmured. 'I bet NASA are having a field day.'

Admiral Bagari, Skateboard and a smattering of officers looked blankly in her direction.

'Y-know? The space people from Earth! With that massive portal hanging right over them they'll probably be running around like headless chickens...bit hard denying the existence of aliens after all of this!'

'Oh please, this is the Earth we are talking about. They couldn't detect a sandwich in a fridge with the crude science they have down there!'

'How are they NOT going to notice that?! A big wibbly-wobbly swirly thing in space?'

'By doing what they always do.' said Admiral Bagari. 'Ignoring the facts staring them in their face! They'll probably even blame it on fake news or something equally as dismissive.'

'Fake what?' said Anji befuddled.

'We have intelligence on your home world, Miss Gummadi,' the Admiral smirked. 'Can't let the human race go unsupervised now, can we? Although you will have to tell me how you come to be this far out in space.'

'Another time,' said Anji defiantly. 'First, we've got to get Random back.'

Random awoke on the floor of his prison cell. Aching, tired, broken.

What he had just been through was like nothing he had ever experienced before. It was all a game to Stratos. He didn't even interrogate them.

Random had no concept of how long he had been lying there but judging by the pool of dribble that lay underneath his mouth, it must have been a little while.

The boy groaned as he pressed his palms down and used them to elevate himself off the floor.

Swinging himself around to sit up, he noticed his friends lying in a similarly undignified fashion, like rag dolls strewn across a play area. He dragged himself to be beside them. Even though they only lay roughly three feet away, the effort Random used to get to them drove him to the edge of exhaustion.

He checked Io first. Her skin was still warm and she appeared to be breathing. Then Jake.

Oh no, what had Stratos done to his best friend?

Random had sworn when he lay recuperating in the hospital bed in the Valetudinarium that he would not put them in danger again.

And once more, he'd failed them.

'Jake, come on, wake up buddy!'

He shook his friend's shoulder vigorously until Jake let out a faint moan.

'Not now Mum, five more minutes please,' he murmured.

Random laughed. 'Oh Jake, even in the darkest times you shine a light on things.'

Jake's eyes opened. His skin was pale and yet dirtied, scorched even, from his ordeal at the hands of Stratos' torture devices.

'How are you feeling mate?' asked Random.
'Like I never want to lick a battery ever again. I haven't been this shocked since a certain someone crashed in a pond on our school trip,' he joked.

'That's two jokes in as many sentences,' remarked Random. 'You must be feeling bad.'

'I've felt better,' Jake agreed as he allowed himself to be pulled upright by his red/blue friend. The pair sat crossed legged, leaning against one another, allowing their life force to slowly flow back through their bodies. With every intake of breath, they felt better.

'Stratos was right,' said Random as he rubbed the back of his neck. 'No long term side effects.'

'Yeah, considering I've been electrocuted for god knows how long, I don't actually feel so bad now I'm awake.'

'We can be thankful of that,' said Random. 'Come on, help me wake Io up.'

'Random, why hasn't he fired on Earth yet? With the other planets he didn't seem to hesitate.'

'Now he's got us he must want us for something.'

'Come on though, if someone hated you that much you'd think they'd kill you straight away. The bloke's only gone and blown up half the galaxy just to get your attention. I mean, why go to all that bother if all he's going to do when he's captured us is give us a little torture with no lingering side effects.'

'I don't know,' mused Random. 'Perhaps he needs me to get home?'

'No,' said a third voice.

It was Io. Unbeknownst to the boys she had already been stirring throughout their conversation. She dragged herself to the opposite side of the cell of her two fellow prisoners.

'He wants to make you watch.'

'Watch? Watch what?'

'The end of the planet you all love so much.'

'The Earth! It's alright I suppose,' said Random.

'There's no suppose about it! We've got to stop him!' cried Jake.

'Calm down, Jake. With any luck Anji and Skate-board will have found help. I mean for all we know they might be constructing a rescue mission right now. Plus if Io's right, he won't blow up the Earth while we are in this cell. He'd want our eyes right on the action…'

Jake shuddered. 'Well, let's do something now before he gets a chance to do it!'

'Not before we find my Mother,' said Io.

Random and Jake looked at one another, both thinking the same thing but daring not to say anything to the girl who had led them into this terrible situation in the first place.

'Io,' said Random tentatively. 'You've got a better view than I have from here. What do you see?'

Io craned her head. Past the wavering wall of energy that fizzed and crackled, holding the three of them in the cramped prison cell, was a corridor leading out of the detention block. She thought to herself how little Stratos must think of their chances with so few guards leering over them!

Just in eyesight, was the shoulder of a Samlore with his back to them, the angle of his arm suggesting he was armed, ready to pounce on the slightest inkling of danger.

'One guard...that's all I can see from here,' she con-firmed.

'I want to test something, so I apologise Io,' said Random.

'Apologise for what?'

'Oh don't give me that! You're the one who led us into this trap. If anything it's your fault, not ours you yellow bellied charlatan!' Random shouted, making Jake jump and Io's mouth flop open in disbelief.

'I'm-sorry,' stammered Io.

'Oh don't give the sob story, sweetheart! You're a filthy turncoat!'

Io ignored the ebbing pains of her electrocution, stomped to her feet and glared down upon Random, her eyes fierce with anger. 'Who are you calling filthy you schbarp!'

Jake gasped.

'I'm presuming that's really rude isn't it?' he said. 'You can shut up too you spotty, smelly adolescent. With a face as punchable as yours no wonder it looks so ugly!'

'Hey!' cried Jake. 'Who are you calling ugly, zit face!' 'Only the girl who has led us to our deaths!' screamed Random. 'You don't deserve to get out of this alive!'

The guard posted at the end of the detention block sighed. It had been a long day. He'd been standing to attention, worried for his life that if he put a clammy paw out of place that his Supreme Leader would crush his skull like an egg for even so much as itching his nose.

He hadn't even been allowed a coffee break.

Now this, a skirmish between the prisoners.

But what if…

No, this couldn't be a ploy to escape now, could it?

'Hey! What's going on back there?' he hollered down the corridor.

'Stay out of this!' came the breaking voice of a teenage boy. 'This is personal!'

'Don't make me come back there…' the guard warned but the commotion was on going. Reluctantly, the guard sighed and allowed himself to be drawn into the argument.

As he made his way towards the chaos, he could hear bits of the cell being thrown about the place.

'Hey! If you break anything in there I'll make you pay for it!' he said as his walk broke into a trot.

As he made it to the cell opening, he could make out that the boy and the girl were tearing chunks out of one another.

'Stop that!' he demanded but it was no use, as Io began to choke Jake in a headlock so hard that his lips were beginning to go blue.

'Right!' cried the Samlore who had no choice but to intervene.

Dropping his weapon to his side, he found the access key in his pocket and swiped it in a slot in the wall. Instantly, the energy wall holding the prisoners in captivity disappeared and the Samlore stepped into the cell.

Then suddenly, that itch he had wanted to scratch went in an instant as a perfect right hook from Random sent his nose flying off his face altogether.

The Samlore was sent hurtling back against the wall, smashing the back of his skull at high-speed impact before leaving a nasty stain trailing down the wall, like a fly having been swatted against a pristine wall, as he slumped unconscious on the ground.

Jake and Io stopped fighting instantly and looked in astonishment at Random, who in turn was staring at his still clenched fist.

'Wow...' said Random. 'Jake...I think my powers are coming back!'

'Never mind that,' said Jake, kicking out at Io as he got up out of the head lock. 'Did you hear what she called me!'

'Oh, like you're faultless in all of this!' said Io, rubbing her shin.

'Well, that's what I am, faultless,' said Jake smugly.

'Tell that to your acne,' she retorted.

'There you go again getting all personal with me!'

'That's so below the belt you're practically kicking me in the-'

'Shut up you two,' implored Random. 'Don't you see? Being electrocuted must have somehow helped me recover a bit of my former strength...do you know what this means?'

'It means you're in with a chance of winning the next series of the Universe's Strongest Man?' said Jake sarcastically, still hurt by the jibes Io had made about his skin.

'It means,' said Random ignoring Jake's last comment, 'that I can take Stratos on! We can beat him!'

'And save my Mother?' asked Io.

'We can do that and more, Io. If my powers are returning then we can stop Stratos and save the entire universe!'

'Great!' said Jake, 'How?'

Random put his arms around their shoulders and drew them closer.

'Here's the plan.'

'What's taking them so long?' Anji's arms were hugged against her stomach, impatiently jostling with Skateboard as the pair waited nervously for an update. They were looking on with invested interest at the conversation Admiral Bagari was having with her fellow Commanders in the Space Seals fleet. They surrounded her, looming large in hologramatic form, with Bagari in the centre, discussing their next move.

'The anomaly has thrown them,' said Skateboard confidently. 'They were expecting to find a battle waiting here for them but instead they've encountered a problem and don't know how to deal with it.'

'So?'

'So, they're soldiers. Killing is easy. Thinking outside the box isn't.'

'But Stratos is sitting there doing nothing!'

'As far as we know, miss.'

'All this time we could be trying to mount a rescue mission.'

'I know,' said Skateboard ruefully. With his ultra-sensitive hearing, he was not only paying full attention to Anji but also the meeting itself.

'What makes it worse is I don't agree at all with what they are proposing to do.'

'What's that then?' asked Anji.

'The council agrees that the presence of a time and space anomaly is unprecedented and this does indeed call for drastic measures,' said one elderly looking officer.

'Add to our current predicament the possibility of other potentially deadly forces that may have escaped from the Beta dimension into ours, this has indeed made things worse,' said another.

'Might I interrupt if I may be so bold?' asked Skateboard.

'You most certainly cannot! snapped Admiral Bagari.

'Is this the prisoner you spoke about, Bagari?' asked a kinder looking lady.

'I'm afraid so,' said Bagari under her breath.

'Then he is the one who discovered the anomaly too?'

'Correct,' said Bagari through gritted teeth. She hated conference calls and hated it even more so when a prisoner she should have thrown in the brig by now was snatching centre stage and undermining her command of the situation.

'Let him speak, er?'

'Skateboard, Admiral,' replied Skateboard.

'Mr Skateboard, what can you tell us about this anomaly. Is it possible that other life has leaked into our universe through it?'

'No, Admiral. From my calculations the structure of the anomaly is not stable enough even for a return visit, let alone repeated passage.'

'How so?' asked the older officer.

'The anomaly was created by a huge explosion on their side of the dimensional rift. And like a paper cut, before long the space around begins to heal itself. The anomaly itself is almost closed but not fully. It needs something a little stronger to repair it.'

'Why not get it a plaster?' said Anji sarcastically. Unsurprisingly, her comment was completely ignored.

'Is it possible that it can be opened again?' asked the kind looking female officer.

'Negative. As soon as the anomaly is shut that is that.'

Bagari smiled. 'So there you have it, my fellow members of the Admiralty. So all we have to do today is seal a tear in the fabric of time and space reality and stop a madman with modified technology powerful enough to destroy planets from doing it again.'

'Admiral, might I make a suggestion?' asked Skateboard confidently.

Admiral Bagari rolled her eyes. 'Go on.'

'Members of the Admiralty, the anomaly is currently 47,000 clicks above the Earth. The Orbital is currently hiding behind the dark side of the moon, but itself is only 8,000 clicks away. If we can attack it and somehow lure it towards the anomaly, then Stratos will perish when the anomaly begins to seal itself. Taking into account the firepower he has at his possession, the explosion would be enough to turn the anomaly into a black hole, sucking the Orbital in and the resulting implosion from that would fold the anomaly in on itself.'

'But doing so will also drag the Orbital out of its hiding place and towards the Earth itself, exposing its presence to the peoples of the Earth to the truth that there is life on other planets,' said the elderly officer. 'Despite there being oblivious to certain expeditions in the past, for them to witness a strategy such as we are planning it could blow the secret out of the water.'

'Sorry, Admiral but it's highly likely they've already spotted it,' said Anji.

'It's risky, very risky,' said another new voice, this time coming from a tall, squid-like looking being. 'It risks dragging the Earth into the fight. They could suffer collateral damage. We must protect them, not put them further at risk.'

'There is also the question of us causing permanent damage to our prize vessel,' said the elderly officer. 'The Orbital is our newest, strongest and most advanced ship in the fleet. If it perishes we face the possibility of weakening the Space Seals resolve.'

'Unfortunately it doesn't look like we have much of a choice,' said the kindly looking Admiral.

Skateboard responded. 'Sir, this Stratos threat is like none we have never faced before. He almost single handedly took the Orbital and killed all of your people on board. I know it's hard but we cannot simply afford any lives to be put at risk by going back there.'

'We could go!' chirped Anji.

'No!' snapped Bagari.

'We are not a part of the Space Seals, and our friends are on board!'

'So you keep saying. But I cannot allow you two to be put at risk. You're civilians.'

'I thought we were prisoners?' questioned Skateboard. 'At least allow us to return to our ship and take part in the attack.'

'What part of, "I won't put your lives at risk" do you not understand?' said Admiral Bagari.

'But we've fought before! And if there's a chance to save our friends we must take it! We can't abandon them to die while you're busy blowing up the ship they are on!' Anji wouldn't relent.

'We have to be careful of the Samlores who are working with Stratos,' said Bagari.

The elderly Admiral groaned. 'Samlores...I should have known they'd be so easily corroborated into working for Stratos. Parasites that they are…'

Anji's frustration was fast reaching breaking point. Random and Jake were alive, she was sure of it, but they wouldn't be for long if they didn't get a move on.

'Do you have experience of combat?' asked one of the hologrammatic Admirals.

'Yes!' cried Anji. 'Without us the people of Genocia would still be slaves. Without us an alien made of sand would have taken over the Earth. And just before we got into this mess we had helped save the people of Spectronia from a race of Egyptian gods!'

'I have to admit,' said the elderly Admiral, 'that is quite a CV. Okay, as long as you are with us then I think you should be allowed to go ahead.'

Despite being granted permission to rush headlong into a deadly situation, Anji couldn't contain her delight.

'Oh thank you, Admiral!'

'Admiral, are you sure?' said Bagari.

'I'd have thought you couldn't wait to get rid of us?' said Anji.

'I'm not a fan of civilians getting caught in the crossfire.'

'Pardon me, Admiral but our friends are trapped over there. This is as much our fight as yours,' said Skateboard.

'Plus we will need to use smaller ships to take on the hornets,' said the squid-like Admiral.

'Hornets?' asked Anji.

'One man fighter ships. They are difficult to lock on to from our guns on board our freighters.'

'We can back you up with some of our own,' said Bagari.

'I can also try to hack into the Orbital's mainframe. I presume that Stratos has changed the codes since he stole it, yes?' asked Skateboard.

'Sadly, yes,' said Bagari.

'Not a problem, I can make a start on hacking in and setting the navigation systems on a trajectory towards the anomaly,' said Skateboard.

'You can do that?' asked Anji.

'Yes, but I need to get closer.'

'Then you could also beam Random and Jake out of there!'

'Oh please, what is your obsession with "beaming up?" Is it an Earth thing?' sniped Bagari.

'You could say that,' said Anji.

'We'd have to get very close to the Orbital to make it even conceivable, miss. I shall work on it simultaneously to hacking the navigation systems and see what I can do.'

'Nice one, Skateboard!' said Anji, the adrenaline was flowing through her body now. Her heart wouldn't stop pumping. 'Well, what are we waiting for, let's go and get them!'

'We'll send the battle freighters in. Top priority is to stop Stratos and protect the Earth. Further written instructions will be sent imminently,' said the elder Admiral. 'This is a message to all Space Seal personnel. Commence battle stations.'

The bright lights on the bridge switched to a dull red and sirens began to wail.

'Get a move on you two!' snapped Bagari. Anji jumped onto Skateboard's back and the pair zoomed out of the bridge.

'We won't just be protecting our universe but making sure that not only is it safer by us doing our duty but that this anomaly, this threat, never happens again,' the elderly Admiral's voice echoed over the alarms.

'So to that end, may we succeed...for all the stars in our galaxies.'

11

THE BEST LAID PLANS...

Back on the Orbital, Random, Jake and Io had met with minimal resistance as they escaped their prison, which struck Random as odd, considering how much Stratos seemed to enjoy tormenting them. Surely, he would have more than just one guard on them at all times? He tried to shake the idea from his head as the trio made for their first destination.

Before they had left the detention centre, Io had insisted that they look for her Mother.

'There's no time!' Random said.

'I'm not going any further until I find her!' Io replied adamantly. Nothing, not even her fear of Stratos and his gang of vile Samlores would shirk her from finding the dearest person to her in the whole universe. 'I'll stay here, you two go on and do what you've got to do.'

'Io, we must stay together if we can. If we don't sabotage Stratos' weapons then the Earth will surely be next. We can't let anyone else perish. Please, do it for Alfragetti. Do it for your Mother.'

Io had given Random and Jake a pleading look. 'Please, just let me check the database for further prisoners. The terminal is just over there.'

Random sighed and nodded. 'You'd better cover her, Jake,' he said without looking at either of his companions.

Io ran across the detention centre floor to a computer bank that jutted out of the wall.

'What if she isn't here?' asked Jake.

'She could be anywhere,' said Random. 'If she is though we can't let another person slow us down so you might have to stay here with them, now go on, cover her.'

Jake saluted and instantly dropped the gun, making a loud metal clunking noise in the process.

'Careful!' Random hissed.

Jake sheepishly picked the gun up, which he had confiscated from the guard they had left without a nose in the prison cell, and shuffled over to Io's side.

He took a glance at the look on her face and thought about asking the obvious.

'Any luck?'

Io's face had fallen.

'No.'

'Chin up. She could be anywhere on this huge ship.'

'She's a prisoner, she should be here!'

'Stratos might be playing mind games with you. He could be playing with all of us,' said Random. 'I'm sorry Io but if she's here we will find her. Please, the Earth is in danger. Help us stop the murder of seven billion people. Come with us.'

Io nodded slowly. 'Yes, alright.'

'Thank you,' Random smiled in appreciation. 'Now then, we need to know how to get to the weapons chamber and a way out of here.'

Random took Io's position in front of the computer bank and started scrolling with his finger on the screen for information.

'So the plan is to sabotage the weapons then get the hell off this ship?'

'That's about the long and the short of it, Jake. If we can carry out as much damage as possible we may be able to disable the Orbital completely.'

'But Stratos would still be alive,' said Io.

'Leave him to me,' replied Random. 'A-ha! Got it!' he cried.

'The armoury is stationed directly 43 decks below us.'

'Great, how do we get down there?' asked Jake.

'Simple,' said Random. 'We take the lift.'

'Oh, that's alright then,' said Jake with relief. 'I thought that you were going to suggest taking the stairs!'

'We have to act fast,' said Random. 'Stratos will know we've gone as soon as that guard comes around.'

'If he ever does,' said Io. 'I have never seen anyone hit with that much power before. Especially from a boy like you.'

'I'm not just any boy,' said Random. 'I'm Random.' 'He certainly is,' said Jake.

'Right come on, let's move out, be aware of any Sam-lores on the way and try to avoid the security cameras whenever you see one! We will be laying a trail but if we work quickly we can keep clear of any conflict.'

The trio left the detention centre and made for the nearest lift, but Jake, who was already heaving the heavy gun around, was already starting to flag a little. Not that he'd ever mention it to the others, of course...he'd already been teased enough for one after-noon!

They made their way down a nondescript grey cor-ridor, which led to another, then another.

'Which way now?' asked Jake as they turned into yet another identical corridor.

'Next left,' said Random.

'Hey, Random?' said jake.

'Yes, mate?'

'Did you mean to hit the Samlores' nose clean off his face?'

'Nope. Just a sign that my powers are coming back. Also that I've had a really bad day.'

They arrived at the lift section and pressed the buzzer. All the time Io could not stop thinking about where her Mother could be. Then she promised herself, if she had the chance, the first sniff of an opportunity, she'd find out for herself, alone if she had to.

And if Stratos had done anything to harm her...then somehow she'd see to the end of Stratos herself...

It wasn't long before they arrived in the weapons chamber, which was bigger than the bridge on the Orbital itself.

'Wow!' Jake had marvelled as he looked up at the sheer vastness of his surroundings.

'Jake!' barked Random.

'Sorry!'

'Zarks. What has he done?' muttered Random as he stood surveying the machinery in front of him.

Towering over them, an array of electrical equipment was bolted together, linked by a complex menagerie of engineering.

'So that's how he's done it!' said Random. 'Stratos has managed to combine all the heavy weaponry on board to make them into one.'

'So that's how he destroyed my home,' said Io.

'Yes, this battle freighter wouldn't have had the capacity to have this form of firepower before he got to it. He's created a doomsday weapon - from scratch!'

'Okay, so he's a genius and a megalomaniac, now come on, let's destroy it!'

'Jake, I don't think you understand. If we blow up this room then the whole ship could go up.'

'So?'

'So will the moon. The devastation it would make would split it into pieces, causing the debris to smash into the Earth.'

Jake's mouth fell open. 'Oh my god, the human race would be extinct! Just like the dinosaurs!'

'The resultant asteroid shower would kill them all,' replied Random.

Jake gulped. 'What do we do?'

'Find the off switch instead. Power the planet destroyer down. Now where is it...' he looked all around the room before lastly taking a look upward into the deep recesses of the huge machine. 'Oh, there it is, right up there.'

Io frowned. 'You can see it from here?'

Elsewhere, the relief guard was idly strolling along the corridor leading to the detention centre to start his shift. He wasn't sure why it was needed, especially after he had witnessed how much they had suffered at the hands of the "lie" detector Stratos had cannibalised into a torture device. But who was he to argue with his Supreme Leader? He'd seen the chaos disobeying his master would bring.

Yet still, he'd taken his sweet time to start his shift. He knew it probably would result in a fight.

Good, he purred.

He loved fights.

As he rounded the corner into the block that held Random and the others, the Samlore was startled.

There was no guard in sight.
The Salmore grinned. He could be useful and report it. He hadn't been useful in a long time.

If ever!

Then he noticed the blood stain on the wall. His eyes followed the trickle of green liquid to the floor, where there appeared to be the end of a Samlores nose. He recoiled. What could have caused such a terrible thing to happen to his comrade? Then he laughed. Somewhere one of his fellow troops was walking around without a nose. Samlores took great pleasure in the hardship of others but they took even greater delight when something terrible happened to one of them!

Being a part of such a twisted race, the Samlore bent down and picked the nose up and raised it to his own. Mockingly, he fastened it to his and then had the terrible image of a Samlore with a heavy cold and two noses and promptly dropped it to the floor again.

As he moved to take his post, he saw something move within the cell.

Of course, the prisoners!
He took a closer look at the shape that was starting to move behind the energy barrier keeping the prisoners inside.

There was only one blur inside.
A blur without a nose.
Without a moment's hesitation, he scrambled back to the command bank and sounded the alarm.

Deep inside the dark recesses of his decimated quarters, Stratos heard the alarm in the split second it began to sound.

His eyes opened and he bolted straight to the door, tearing his recharge socket out of his shoulder and the wall simultaneously. His metallic teeth gnashed together and bit down hard. The anger and rage began to boil within his bionic body.

Stratos knew what the alarm meant.
He also knew the first place they would go...

Down in the weapons chamber, Random, Jake and Io jumped as the sound of the alarm blared over the ebb and flow of the sounds made by the pulsing weaponry.

Random turned on his toes. 'Right, you two! Head to the spacecraft hangar and get yourselves out of here.'

'We can't leave you!' cried Jake.

'We can't leave my Mother!' replied Io.

'Listen to me, both of you. I can't reach the off

switch in time. I need to work out how to sabotage this thing just enough so it doesn't cause another disaster.'

'Fine!' said Jake, 'but when we do find a ship, I'll keep the engine ticking over until you get there.'

'No you won't, I must stay here to make sure Stratos does not escape. Go now!'

'But...'

'Come on!' said Io as she took Jake's arm and began to drag him away from his friend.

Random watched as his friends left the chamber and disappeared out of the room. He took a sharp in-take of breath and looked up at the colossal magnitude of the weaponry system.

'How to break it but not blow us sky high...'

'Red group leader, standing by!'

'Blue group leader, standing by!'

'Gold group leader, standing by!'

'Venus II, standing by!'

Now that the call signs were out of the way, Anji and Skateboard were ready for take-off.

'Right, Skateboard, what would you like me to do?' asked Anji as she fastened the seat belt in her co-pilot's chair.

'Nothing that I can think of, miss. I believe I have complete control of the ship and the means as to which enable us to engage in combat.'

'Well, I'm not sitting here doing nothing, come on, there's got to be something I can do to help?'

Skateboard's diodes whirred.

'I don't suppose you've ever had any experience prior to our meeting of firing a weapon?'

'Yeah,' Anji's eyes lit up. 'Plenty!'

'Good, then let me show you how to work our weapons systems.'

He paused.

'I was not aware that children on Earth were allowed to use firearms?'

'Yeah, course we were, I used to shoot things all the time back home.'

Skateboard's curiosity was well and truly stirred.

'Really? Where was that then? On a shooting range?'

'Nah. PlayStation.'

'ALL UNITS PREPARE TO DISEMBARK.'

A voice piped over the speaker system into the huge spacecraft hangar.

The room was a hive of activity. Swathes of Space Seals had rushed into their crafts while others in over-alls worked as quickly as possible to finish fuelling and arming them, who were now running full pelt to clear the runways and leave the area. The Space Seals called their fighter crafts "Hornets" after the Earth insect of the same name, which had led Anji to question just how they had so much information on her home world.

The ships themselves were only big enough for the pilot, small in shape and slight in design with a huge sting protruding out of the front of it, just below the view screen.

Two tiny wings either side hummed loudly making the hangar echo with the sound of a swarm.

The Hornets were black in colour, all except for the pattern at the front, distinguishing which group leader it and its fighter pilot had been assigned to. Like hornets themselves it was waspish, quick in the air and if provoked, deadly.

'That's the order, get ready, Skateboard, hold on to your wheels!'

'FIVE.'

'I feel as though you're getting quite a thrill from all of this, miss.'

'FOUR.'

'Really?' she winked.

'THREE.'

'I wonder what gave that away?'

'TWO.'

'I just want my friends back, Skateboard.'

'So do I, Anji,' he chirped. 'So do I.'

ONE

'Well then shall we?'

The hangar door burst open and with a collective explosion of noise and fire, the Venus II, followed by the sound of dozens of engines roared into life tore off the tarmac and shot out into space, closely followed by the swarm of Hornets.

The blackness of space became a wash of red, blue and gold colour as the swarm burst out the battle freighter like a nest. As they did, more swarms pierced into space and joined up with those that erupted first.

Then another exploded from a third battle freighter and the Hornets settled into triangular formation, with the Venus II at the point and behind them four of the battle freighters also formed a solid wall of defense.

Back on Admiral Bagari's bridge, the officers on board paced up and down noisily setting about their preparation for attack.

'Ma'am, the battle force confirms it is in formation,' said the Parropus.

Admiral Bagari, sat imperially in her command chair, clicked a switch on the arm control panel.

'Bagari to the Swarm...take us in.'

On the command, the Venus II and the Hornets shot off from their present location, closely followed by the battle freighters towards the Orbital…

Meanwhile, Jake and Io had reached the spaceship hangar.

As they entered the area, Io stopped on her heels. 'Io,' Jake huffed. 'What are you doing?'

'My Mother, I can't leave her here!'

'Io, they know we are here, we've got to go!'

'Not without her!'

Jake turned back and ran towards her.

'Listen to me. Random is smarter and stronger than he looks. He will save her, I'm sure of it. Now let's get out of here.'

Io paused and watched as Jake tore off towards one of the multitude of Hornets that sat with their cockpit hatches open. She spotted the hangar door. It was shut.

'He's not as clever as you make him out to be,' she sighed. 'Someone has to open that to let you out.'

Jake turned and just heard her over the alarm siren. 'Io, I know we might have got off on the wrong foot, but'

'Just get out of here, you silly little boy. Don't worry about it, honestly. I got you into this mess. By getting you out of it, we can call it quits.'

Jake sighed. He hadn't the time to argue with her. 'Are you sure you know how to do it?'

'No more than you probably do flying that thing!'

She had a point. Jake took a peep inside the hatch. He saw a steering wheel, two big buttons and a pull lever.

'Seems easy enough,' he shouted back. 'You'll need this!' he sprinted back to her and gave her his gun. He stood silently, panting for breath, trying to wish her luck.

'You too,' she said. Io gave Jake a tiny peck on his cheek. 'And I'm sorry, now go!'

Jake did just that. He pelted back to the Hornet as Io ran to the control box directly in the middle of the hangar. She familiarised herself with the controls and noticing a huge lever, surmised that that must be for the hangar doors.

She watched as Jake pulled himself inside the Hornet. When inside, he pulled the lever and the hatch snapped shut.

'Right, I passed that test then,' he said to himself as he heard the sound of the huge metallic hangar door start to snap itself open. He looked down on the two big buttons. Now in theory, he thought to himself, one of these is the start-up button and the other is the one that fires the lasers. He hovered over the button to the left and then decided to press the right one. A barrage of laser fire exploded out of the sting at the front of his craft and promptly blew the Hornet in front of him into pieces.

'Ah,' he cried and gave a nervous grin to Io in the command box, who herself was covering her face in terror.

Jake pressed the other button with all his might and the engine burst into life. Using the logic he had recently acquired on his flying lesson in the Venus II, he pulled the steering column up and the Hornet noisily rose into the air. He smiled a big dopey grin.

'I'm a space pilot!'
With one final shot, and a fairly cheesy salute to Io, Jake pulled the steering column forward and the Hornet shot out into space and away from danger.

Io pushed the lever back down again and raced back into the corridor. She ran as fast as her legs would carry her, gun in hand, looking for an information port. Luckily she found one quickly, the sound of the alarms throbbing inside her skull. Desperately, she did what she could to blot it out of her mind as her focus fixed solely back to her Mother.

She searched for lifeforms on board. There were not many.

There were nearly a dozen Samlores.

One metal machine.

Two organic creatures.

Then her heart sank.

Only one of them was an Alfrajetti.

Herself.

Io's eyes began to flood with tears. She blinked hard and they trickled down her face. A great pool of emotions engulfed her. Grief, Anger.

Stratos had lied to her.

He hadn't saved her Mother.

Io swore knew the truth now.

As she collapsed to the ground, allowing the tidal wave of loss wash over her, she hugged herself as she cried out loud.

She was all that was left of the Alfrajetti.

Stratos had killed her too.

How could she have been so stupid?

Io had been used.

It was the sound of the weaponry chamber door blowing open that Random heard first. He swore to himself. Unable to sabotage without causing a massive explosion, he'd decided to try and climb up to switch the weapons off. He was only three quarters of the way up the huge scape of the doomsday weapon and nowhere near the shutdown switch and he'd already been discovered.

A gaggle of Samlores burst into the room and took a look around.

'There!' cried the Commander who spotted Random doing his best Spider-Man impression far up above them.

With one word, he gave the command for his soldiers to fire. They assumed their positions, raised their weapons and sent a volley of laser fire crashing all around Random. He did his best to avoid them but with his back to the attack, he was stuck.

The hulking frame of Stratos crashed through what was left of the entrance to the chamber and glared upwards.

'Stop! You'll kill us all!' he commanded, swiping a Samlore clean off his feet in the process. The Samlores ceased fire.

He glared at the far-off image of Random continuing his ascent.

'He's mine...'

With a mighty spring from his powerful legs, Stratos propelled himself high into the air.

Random looked behind him and his eyes grew wide in terror as his nemesis hurtled towards him.

Before he had time to act, Stratos landed a mighty punch square on Random's jaw, forcing the boy's head to brutally smash into the metal housing that he was climbing up. Involuntarily, Random lost his grip and started to fall, only to be caught by Stratos instantly.

Before long Stratos, with Random being held by his t-shirt dangling at his side, landed firmly back on the ground. The Samlores felt the force of the landing and the vibration sent those nearest to the impact centre falling to the floor.

'Fire up the device,' yelled Stratos to the Commander as he strode out of the chamber. Random, too groggy to put up a fight, dangled within his grasp, trying to collect his thoughts. As they left the room, Stratos smashed the alarm button with his free hand.

As the Samlores filed out of the chamber, the alarm was silenced and the weaponry chamber fell back into its usual hum of energy.

But where the laser fire had burrowed into the doomsday weapon, the metal, unnoticed by all in the room, was starting to buckle ever so slightly...

Jake screamed out loud as the Hornet wobbled and jutted. Although he had felt fairly confident about flying a spacecraft, he quickly realised that his inner bravado was ever so slightly misplaced. For a start, in the recent past he'd had Skateboard sitting beside him, guiding him with every misjudged acceleration of late breaking, but there was no AI robot with him now. He couldn't even see the break!

As he wrestled with the controls something strange struck him. The Orbital wasn't firing on him. Either Random had succeeded in his sabotage of the doomsday weapon or maybe, just maybe, Stratos and his cronies hadn't noticed that he had slipped out.

Come to think of it, he hadn't seen many of those horrible looking Samlores when he had been held captive. On a ship of that size, he'd have thought it would have taken a whole army to abduct a battleship. But no. It was only Stratos who had done it.

He didn't want to let on but his encounter with the terrorist had really unsettled him. His callousness, the unfeeling way in which the cyborg had tortured them. Jake had never been tortured before. He'd never come up against a man of such brutish capabilities.

It had hurt him. Deeply.

He tried to shake the thoughts from his mind as he continued to pilot the little Hornet the best he could. He dare not look behind him so putting the pedal to the metal Jake shot the Hornet away from the Orbital as fast as it would go. As the cockpit juddered and shook, Jake looked out of the view screen and tried to get a fix on where he was going. He could see a huge greyish moon to his right that swamped his sight so he concentrated on the little bit of starry space that was just past it.

And as he did, he thought that he saw something. No, not something, several things.

More than that, lots of somethings!

As they got closer, Jake recognised what was he was flying towards.

It was a full on armada in space.

Dozens of Hornets, just like the one he had commandeered, were growing larger before him. Following them was what looked like large slabs of grey but it was the ship that was way out in front, with its sleek silver finish that brought the biggest smile to Jake's lips.

It was the Venus II. His home!

'This is Admiral Bagari of the Space Seals Corp. Please state your name and intent.'

Jake began to scream. 'It's me! Anj, Skateboard!'

'I shall ask again. Please state your name and intent.'

Jake took a look around. They could not hear him.

'Uh…'

'If you do not co-operate we will be forced to take offensive action.'

'Woah, alright alright!' he started waving. 'I don't mean any harm!'

Suddenly a more familiar, friendly voice broke over the speakers.

'Random?'

'I don't think they can hear us, miss,' said another familiar, more robotic voice. 'I'll patch into the comm system.'

A blaring distortion exploded over the airwaves, making Jake put his hands over his ears and lose control of the Hornet. It began to barrel roll towards the fleet.

'He's attacking us!' cried Bagari.

'No!' scream Anji.

Jake grappled with the steering wheel and eventually brought the Hornet back under what little control he had.

'Bloody hell,' cursed Jake.

'Jake!' Anji sounded absolutely relieved as she heard the voice of her friend. 'Admiral, it's Jake, don't shoot!'

'Then why is he in attack mode?' came the unimpressed Bagari.

'Uh, sir, ease off on the accelerator if you would be so kind?' asked Skateboard.

Jake did as he was told and instantly the Hornet became more controllable.

'I take it that's why you have the stabilisers on when you let him fly the Venus?' said Anji on the sly.

'You leave the stabilisers on?' said a rather indigent Jake.

'Never mind about that, get out of the way!' cried Bagari. 'You're directly in the path of our battle fleet!'

'Guys,' said Jake ignoring the Admiral's order. 'Random and Io are still on board. He's got this weapon...he's going to use it on Earth! Random's trying to sabotage it right now...that's if he didn't get him.'

'Stratos?' said Anji.

'Anj, he's evil. Like, really evil. We've got to stop him.'

'We will if you get out of the way!' Bagari was starting to get a little exasperated. First the talking robot had shown her up in front of her peers, now some teenage boy was stalling possibly her greatest moment in the field.

'I'm going to help.'

'Then stay where you are and we'll come and get you,' said Skateboard.

'Nope. I want to fight in this thing.'

'Seriously?' said Anji, Skateboard and Bagari all at the same time.

'Yeah, I feel like I've got the hang of it.'

'You'll be much safer here, sir.'

'No, I want to do my bit to stop him.'

Back on board the Orbital, Random was strung up in the restraints once more as the Samlores prepared him for torture. Slumped and barely with it, Random tried to prepare himself for more of the anguish he had been forced to endure.

If his theory was correct, it was going to be the only thing that would ensure that he would defeat Stratos once and for all.

'Supreme Leader, we are ready to move the Orbital towards the target.'

'Good.'

The Orbital began to sway as his huge engines began to slowly pull the gigantic battle freighter out of its hiding place.

Stratos paced up and down the bridge. His anger was barely brimming underneath the surface. He had Random back in the torture device, barely conscious.

'Captain, you didn't have to go to all of this trouble. If you liked my therapy you only needed to ask for more.'

He grabbed Random by the hair and forced him to look his nemesis in the eyes.

'We won't want you missing the fireworks either now, will we?'

Random coughed. 'Why...the-'
'The Earth? Well it's always been your favourite planet. No matter which dimension this may be, the third rock from the sun has always been a jewel in the eye of the butcher of the cosmos. That's why you protected it so viciously. I've never seen you care so much for anything more than you do that miserable little planet.'

'But...you don't know me, Stratos.'
'But I do! And although my plans have altered some-what since I came here I thought it would be rude not to complete what I was destined to do and then go home.'

'Bet you can't...'
Stratos paused.
'What did you say?' Random
smiled. 'You heard.'

Stratos strode up to his captive and smashed his face with a swipe of his back hand.

'Explain what you mean by that.'

Random reeled. That hurt. That hurt big time. But he was well past the pain threshold to stop now.

'Either/or.'

Stratos looked at Random furiously.

'How did you know?'

'Know what?'

'That I can't go back.'

'I didn't,' said Random. 'You just told me.'

Stratos pulled his backhand down on Random yet again, the savage blow nearly knocking him out of his restraints.

'It will be good to get you from underneath my skin,' spat Stratos. 'Yes, I located the anomaly that brought me here. And when I saw that it had appeared above Earth, I thought it good to destroy that vacuous rock and its stupid lifeforms before going home and doing exactly the same on the other side. Two universes. No human race.'

'Lemme guess,' Random spluttered. 'A one-way ticket?'

'If anything tries to enter it from this side it will be torn apart and the anomaly will close.'

'And poor old Stratos can never go home. Face it, you're stranded.'

Stratos thumped his fist through a control terminal.

'You've always talked too much,' he raced over to the torture device, pushed the Samlore operating it clean out of the way and set it to full.

A shock of lightning cascaded out of the impulses digging into Random's brain and the brilliant flash of blue flooded the bridge as the boy began to writhe and scream in agony.

'Not for much longer. You'll be kept in a state of perpetual torment for as long as I see fit. And when your precious Earth is nothing but dust, you'll be no more.'

Stratos roared maniacally as Random did his best to stay awake and absorb the pain.

If he could, if his strength would allow, harness it.

Stratos turned to look outside and he gazed upon the blue/green planet that had begun to hone into view.

High above it, and not far away from the Orbital at all, was the swirling image of the anomaly.

It should have been his gateway home.

Now it hung there in space, teasing him.

Playing with what was left of his heart.

A reminder of what once was.

But now he could make this universe his. Nothing was going to stop him.

'Sir!' came a cry from the Commander. 'There's a fleet of ships coming in hot.'

Stratos tore himself away from the screen.

'How many?'

'Four battle freighters, thirty Hornets and a ship I don't recognise, Supreme Leader.'

Stratos peered into the monitor.

'I do,' he spat. All too well.

It was the Venus II.

'Commander, I want all of you to go out there and stall them.'

The Commander gulped. 'But Supreme Leader, they outnumber us.'

'I don't care, go!'

The Commander didn't budge. Not out of insubordination, but out of fear.

'NOW!'

He jumped to it and began to rally the small group of Samlores on the bridge together.

'You heard our Supreme Leader, every Samlore to the hangar, now!'

Random just about heard the commotion. And although his screams had died down as he was becoming too weak to even cry out in agony, Stratos was provoked further by his prisoner as Random emitted a little smile.

Disbelieving at how she had been manipulated, Io wiped the tears across her face with her sleeve as she walked slowly back towards the weaponry chamber. Suddenly, she heard footsteps growing nearer. She instantly ducked inside a crescent and hid from view as she witnessed what must have been every Samlore on board tearing down the corridor back the way she came. When the commotion had passed, she took a cautious look from her hiding spot and when she thought it was safe, continued on her journey.

Far below, a little girl was practising her shots with her basketball, whilst waiting for her friend from the next block over to where she lived with her Mum in Brooklyn to meet with her. Despite being only eight, she had convinced her only parent that she was big enough to play outside by herself, but had settled on the compromise that it was fine as long as she agreed a time and a place to meet and did not come home any later than the curfew time.

Happily, the girl grabbed her basketball, which was still slightly too big for her and tore off across the busy street to the local park. The weather wasn't exactly the best on this particular day in New York but the windy weather didn't bother her. The sun was still shining and for once, the court was empty.

She hadn't been exactly straight with her Mum and had gone out to play ten minutes earlier than her friend to practice shooting hoops. Who knows, one day she may even throw the ball high enough to get it through the hoop!

Of course she would. Everyone in the NBA had started out somewhere.

As she dribbled with severe concentration, she picked the ball up and threw it without looking where she was chucking it.

She did it.

She made the hoop.

The ball trickled tantalisingly around the rim and actually dropped through the net.

The little girl should have been ecstatic but she didn't see it.

The spaceship in the sky had distracted her.

Dexter Mackay was having a bad day. Not only was the office a state, but his dreams of getting his recycling plan off the ground lay in tatters, much like the rubbish that had been accumulating in Hyde Park over the last few months.

His idea was foolproof. It had gone through the planning stages no problem. It was cheap, clean and easy to put in place.

Plus it had a snazzy slogan.

DON'T BE A LITTER BUG. PICK IT UP.

Or so he thought.

Maybe that's where he had lost the interest of his fellow MPs in the cabinet meeting. They'd been all about slogans of late.

But now that the Prime Minister had flatly denied him his chance, he was in a funk. Although it was late at night, he couldn't sleep. His office chair was too lumpy and there was no chance his wife would let him in the house at this hour. Especially if it meant waking her up as he'd left his keys at home again.

Rubbing his eyes, Dexter picked up the cold take-away and walked over to the window. He expected to see nothing but the busy streets of London. In particular, the bright lights and the throngs of people going about their Friday nights along the River Thames. But everyone was standing still. Looking upward.

Up until then, to Dexter there was nothing happening out of the ordinary.

Nothing except for the huge spaceship that appeared to now be hanging in the sky.

As the people of Earth should have been waking up or going to bed or going about their business, events occurring hundreds of miles above them were about to take place...and the fate of them all was hanging by a thread...

12

THE BATTLE FOR THE SOLAR SYSTEM

The Samlores were like lambs sent to the slaughter. The Commander knew it. But whatever they did now, they were dead. If they disobeyed their Supreme Leader's order, he'd have annihilated all of them before they had a chance to mount an attack. No matter how futile.

As he led his small band of troops towards the on-coming storm that was the Space Seals battle fleet, some how he felt content with his fate.

There was nothing he could do. If they ever so much as attempted a runner, the Space Seals would catch up with them in an instant. If they went back, they'd have the wrath of Stratos to contend with.

They were his decoy.

He only needed them to buy him a little time. So
that was what they were going to give him. Not for
Stratos.
But for them.
What little honour they had.

Back on Admiral Bagari's battle freighter, the Parro-
pus officer had spotted the enemy Hornets approaching the
fleet.
'Targets are in sight,' he said.
'Shields up. Hornets...on my mark,' said Bagari. Just a
little closer.
And then something happened that startled her. She left
it too long.
One of the enemy Hornets fired, taking out one of the
Space Seals own, right next to the Venus II.

*

Anji cried out in shock.
'Skateboard, that wasn't Jake's was it?'
'I'm still here, Anj,' came a voice over the speakers. The
Samlores had blinked first.
Bagari took her microphone in her grasp.
'Fire!'
And with that, the battle for the solar system began.

The Samlores had little to no battle tactics. They flew

all over the place, no formation and opened fire wherever they liked.

The Venus II looped the loop and attempted to chase one of the enemy Hornets down but the craft was elusive, fast.

Jake flew his own craft to be close to his friends and in doing so narrowly missed being blown sky high by a volley of fire from the nose of a Samlore that had clearly had its eyes on him. But the Space Seals pilots were impeccable in their co-ordination and one of their own immediately blasted the Samlore out of the sky.

'Let them get on with it!' cried Bagari, who spotted that the Orbital was now within firing range of the Earth. 'All freighters, all freighters, engage the Orbital.'

The battle freighters moved on, letting the Hornets clear up the mess that their fight with the Samlores was creating.

'Skateboard, please tell me that you have hacked into their navigation computer already?' there was an element of nervousness in Bagari's voice.

*

Back on the Venus II, not only was Skateboard doing his best to tail the Hornet which had provoked him, but he was also still trying to hack the mainframe on the Orbital.

'Almost there, Admiral,' he said, lying slightly.

Of the possible 96,489 combinations that he had calculated, he'd only attempted 13,592 so far but at least one of his objectives was almost complete. Within moments, he was done.

'The Orbital's shields are powering down,' he declared before turning to his co-pilot.

'Miss, ready when you are,' he said, buying enough time to attempt another couple of thousand.

Without replying, Anji fired the laser cannons and obliterated the Hornet.

'Good shooting, girl!' said Jake, who in watching his friends in battle had completely failed to notice a Samlore on his port side, half on fire, but still capable of taking him out.

Anji had noticed his predicament but it was too late. To his surprise, Jake's Hornet was sent spiraling out of control as the Samlore rammed him, embedding the gun sting at the front into his cockpit, sending both ships cartwheeling off into space.

*

The first thing that Io saw was the huge doomsday weapon. The instrument that destroyed her home planet. She readied her gun and leveled it up at the vast housing that held it in place and saw the stress and strain of the buckled metal.

'Looks like Random's left the rest to me,' she said to herself.

She thought of Alfrajetti. She thought of her family. She thought of her Mother.

'This one's for you, Mum.'

Random blinked his eyes open, his jaw throbbing red hot. Stratos must have brought him around with another savage blow. But he didn't mind. The pain would not be permanent. Any moment now, the tables would be turning.

'I thought it would be a pity if you missed this,' said Stratos, who loomed over the command port, cold metal fingers poised over the red button.

Smiling sinisterly he relished the moment.

This was going to be a moment to savour.

But something didn't feel right.

'No final pleas for me to stop, Captain?'

'You've gotta do what you've gotta do,' Random rasped, his throat dry as sawdust.

'I want to see the look in your eyes as the Earth burns…'

Stratos pressed the button.

*

Far below on Earth, the human race collected together, watching the strange and slightly scary vision of a
spaceship hover high in the sky.

But no-one ran and nobody panicked.
Instead they stood there and watched the fate of their
world play out...mainly through their camera phones…

*

Nothing happened.
Stratos pressed the button again.
The same outcome.
Something very wrong had occurred.
Instead of the sound of a magnificent explosion and
the brilliant light of destruction flooding his field of vision,
Stratos could only hear the hum of the ship's engines. Then
came a sound that made him even angrier than he had ever
been before.
The sound of a boy laughing.
'What have you done?' he demanded.
Random's laugh was becoming more vigorous by the
second.
Stratos' black eyes looked Random square in the
face.
Random stared back at his enemy and tried suc-
cessfully to stop.

'It's nothing I've done, your lab rats fired on the weapon system, not me!'

'No,' said Stratos. 'It can't be! It can't be!'

'Oh, I'm afraid it is. This is what happens when you enlist the help of mercenaries. They were never your soldiers, Stratos. They were just idiots with guns.'

Stratos hollered out in sheer frustration. He went over to the security terminal and punched his fist clean through the image on the screen.

'The girl…' he spat.

Random stopped laughing instantly. 'No…' Suddenly the ship jolted. Random pulled at his manacles. Io must have stayed on board, he thought to himself. He had to stop her. She'd caused the doomsday weapon to fail. He had to stop her as much as Stratos did. One false shot would blow them all sky high.

What's more, he had to save her…

'Stratos, we have you surrounded.'

A new voice bled into the bridge.

'This is Admiral Bagari of the Space Seals Corp. You have taken our vessel and committed genocide. We will give you ten seconds to surrender. Lower your shields and turn yourself over.'

'NO!' screamed Stratos. He spotted Random trying to break free and thrust himself into the torture device's instruments and threw it into maximum. Random immediately stopped what he was doing and began to writhe in pain again.

Bagari's voice boomed once more. 'Stratos, we have hacked into your mainframe. Your shields are down and your weapons are offline. You have five seconds…'

But Stratos wasn't listening. He had to get the doomsday weapon functioning again.

'Four…'

Stratos had left the bridge. It was only Random, screaming in agony left. Despite the torment, he was straining at his bonds…

'Three…'

As the bolts of lightning continued to riddle his body, Random grimaced as the manacle holding his right arm in place snapped…

'Two…'

There went the one holding his left leg down…

'One…'

With one herculean effort, Random exploded out of his bonds, tore the helmet off his head and threw it to the floor. As he jumped through the air, the first volley of fire from the battle freighters smashed into the side of the Orbital, sending sparks and jets of smoke cascading out everywhere.

Random didn't allow it to distract him.

He had his strength back.

The torture had the opposite effect - it had made him better again.

Without a moment to lose, Random sped his way af-ter Stratos towards the weaponry chamber.

There was one more life to save today…

*

The sound of Jake screaming bounced around the walls of the cockpit as Anji and Skateboard chased his ship. There was not much left of the battle. The Space Seals had obliterated the Samlores, but one ship was proving elusive and had set off in hot pursuit of the Venus II.

Bloodied and wounded, the Commander sneered as he set his sights on the silver pearl in the black of space.

'Er...Skateboard…'

'Sorry, miss, I'm a little busy with this final code…' said Skateboard, who was just one thousand combinations from sending the Orbital hurtling into the anomaly. Despite his capability to do any number of things at one time, he was adamant he needed to dedicate as much of his concentration on this final task as possible.

The Commander raised his sighter and prepared to fire.

'Anji…' said Skateboard, with just five combinations left. 'Six o'clock…'

Anji looked perplexed. Then she remembered her job. Instantly, she swung her laser gun towards the blip on their scanner and fired.

The Commander, who had his finger on the button, had no time to press it as his Hornet exploded into a million pieces.

'Excellent shot, miss,' said Skateboard.

The final combination had been cracked.

He switched off the audio of Jake, who by now sounded like he was throwing up, and made contact with the battle fleet.

'Admiral Bagari, I'm in.'

Bagari grinned. 'Send him to hell…'

*

Back on board the Orbital, Stratos' bionic legs had powered him way ahead of Random and he sprinted back into the weaponry chamber.

It was a complete mess.

Shards of blasted metal and plastic lay strewn all over the place. The ship jolted again as the battle fleet continued its relentless attack, causing more explosions all over the ship.

'What have you done!?' he cried…the room apparently empty of other life.

Suddenly a blast shot Stratos in his back. It did little but to singe him where other men it would have burrowed clean through.

Stratos turned and spotted Io, shivering in the shadows.

As he advanced, she shot again. Once more, the bolt deflected off him. The same thing happened again and again, until Stratos snatched the gun from her grasp, snapped it in two and picked her up by the throat.

Io's face turned blue as her eyes began to pop out of their sockets.

'To think I nearly saved your Mother...you just weren't quick enough...'

Stratos squeezed his grip.

And with that Io's eyes flickered shut.

Random bolted down the corridor and could see the silhouette of Stratos holding Io's lifeless body up against the flames.

'No!' he cried as he tore straight into Stratos' midriff, sending Io's body tumbling to the ground and Stratos himself flying like a bullet into the wall, where he almost tore a hole through it.

Random scrambled to Io's body but he was just too late. His eyes began to well up. Not another life…

The roar of Stratos hurtling towards him took his glaze away from Io's pale face. The force of him tearing him away and throwing him down the corridor sent him reeling. He regrouped quickly and threw as good as he got back at the metal monster. He landed a punch full on Stratos' jaw and sent him sprawling.

Stratos looked down. Blood was pouring from his mouth. Black, tar-like blood.

'Finally...some guts...' he jibed as he sent a devastating blow right back at Random, who ducked and sped around the back of Stratos, punching with all his might, denting Stratos' monstrous body.

He had to keep going. Punching and kicking. Ignoring the fire around him as the Orbital continued to buckle under the strength of the battle fleet's assault. He had to stop Stratos here and now.

Even if it meant the death of him, too.

*

Jake's eyes stopped spinning. Retching again, he had no more to give. Falling back to the floor, his stomach ached. Looking around, he was dismayed at what he had done to the decor of the cramped vessel.

'Jake, are you alright?'
'Anj...I'm fine. Just give me a few minutes to regroup and possibly hose myself down and I'll be right with you.'

'I've got the ship's laser triggered on the Hornet. You might want to hold onto something...'

'Oh no!' cried Jake. 'Please, not again!'

Meanwhile, on board the Hornet that had embedded itself inside Jake's cockpit, the Samlore, now the last surviving Samlore in the whole solar system, had similarly stopped himself from vomiting at the sheer velocity of the spinning Hornets and looked up to see nothing but the side of his enemies craft. He noticed the gun was embedded in the cockpit. So, all it would take was one shot and his enemy would be blasted out of the sky and he would be free.

Unfortunately for him, Anji was just too quick. With a squeeze of her trigger, the Samlore was no more and once again, Jake's craft was sent spinning into space.

'We'd better go and pick him up...when he's stopped of course,' said Skateboard.

'How's the rest of it going?'
Anji looked up as the Venus II's scanner showed her the current events.

The Orbital was sailing closer and closer to the anomaly and a barrage of fire was exploding from the four battle freighters and blowing chunks out of it.

'I suppose you're going to say that we can't fly in and help Random, aren't you?' Anji said.

'If we fly into the carnage we risk being hit ourselves. If we get too close to the anomaly we also risk being pulled in by its gravitational field. I'm sorry, but we've done what we can, miss,' said Skateboard. 'It's up to Random now.'

A light bulb went off in Anji's head.

'We've still got to save him...and you know what, Skateboard? I know exactly how we can do it...'

More and more debris began to tear away from both the interior and exterior of the massive battle freighter. At Admiral Bagari's command the Space Seals threw more aggression at a ship that was once theirs, but now they were willing to sacrifice it to destroy the threat that it carried. As it lurched closer and closer to the anomaly, two enemies fought it out on board.

*

Random's super speed was back and although Stratos was able to land blow after blow upon his frame, he had been able to counter attack. Punch after punch and kick after kick sent them sprawling into their surroundings, further damaging the internal structure of the Orbital. Random and Stratos had torn whole chunks out of it and each other.

As the fight moved onto a high rise of pathways and corridors that dangled high above nothingness, Stratos fell back over a precipice and crunched through the floor of a walkway below. In doing so, he tore a massive part of his chest plate off.

Random leapt down to join him but spotted from a distance the exposed wiring and broken circuitry of a cyborg who was surely now on the edge of complete failure.

Random landed a clean right hook squarely in the eye socket of the creature who had claimed so many lives just to spite an enemy who in this universe he didn't even possess.

Stratos cried out as the punch knocked him free of his grasp on the walkway and he fell further below.

But Random wasn't finished yet. He dived after him immediately, caught him by the exposed chest unit and began to punch and tear at anything he could. They seemed to plunge towards doom for ages before the back of Stratos finally broke their fall against the very bottom of the ship. The force of the crash sent an echo that even the silence of space would have heard. Random tumbled to the ground, panting, bleeding all over. He craned his neck to see Stratos, his circuitry wheezing, all that was human still groaning and crying out in agony. He was broken, again, at the hands of his worst enemy.

'It's shocks me to hear that you still feel,' said Random as he rolled onto his front. Both adversaries were moving gingerly, defying the injuries and damage they had both sustained.

'You think that you are better than me?' growled Stratos, his voice sounding broken. 'That compassion and valor set us apart. You're wrong Captain. I've seen what you are capable of. I KNOW what you can do. In defeating you I had to become like you. But I've seen what happens to Captain Random when he succumbs to temptation. To evil. Believe me, in killing you I'd be saving your pitiful universe!'

'You're wrong, Stratos. I've seen temptation. I've looked right into its green envy and I rejected it. Right there and then. I allowed it to consume me and it very nearly destroyed me. But I'm never making that mistake again.'

Random grabbed Stratos by the throat.

Stratos choked and then began to laugh.

'But I have won,' he coughed. 'Because I've brought you down to my level...you're willing to kill to protect...don't you think that's what I had to do?'

'I really don't care what you had to do,' said Random, tightening his grip. 'This isn't your universe. You have no say over what it does. Because of your monstrous terrorism billions of lives have been lost. The universe won't ever forgive you and it sure as hell will never forget.'

Stratos grinned a sickening smile. 'Then I really have won...and the best part of it all? You die in the fire with me.'

Random frowned.

'This ship is falling into the anomaly...in a few minutes we will be nothing but a memory...an indelible one, stained across the cosmos. What a victory...' Stratos croaked, black blood oozing out of his mouth.

Random looked around him. He'd been so wrapped up in his wrath that he had failed to notice that the ship was indeed falling apart and had felt like it was being pulled against its will. He thought it had been the gunfire from the Space Seals, but he was wrong.

'Someone must have hacked your navigation system,' he mused. Then he smiled, 'Skateboard!'

Random leaned in so that his face was right up against his foe. One of Stratos' eyes had burst and the other was still as black as its owner's heart.

'Sorry, Stratos, but this ride has room for one person only…'

He let go of his enemy, letting him tumble back and walked towards some hanging debris. If it could support his weight for just a couple of seconds, he could hop his way back up to the top of the ship and then leg it back to the bridge. But the walls had begun warping all around him, buckling as the dimensional strain of the anomaly was beginning to suck the Orbital into its void.

Stable for a moment on the remains of a gantry, Random yearned to have the final say in this horrible fight. 'You know what your biggest failure was, Stratos? Your ego. You tried to do it all yourself and look where it got you. Your weapons sabotaged, the ship defenseless, your minions useless and wiped out in an instant and now you're plunging into oblivion. I have my friends and I know that they will always, ALWAYS have my back.'

The Orbital began to warp out of shape, buckling and screaming as it twisted and snapped.

'You got distracted and it cost you. The chaos you create means nothing to the chaos that has been your downfall. Normally I'd have some shred of compassion for my enemies but you, you've deserved everything you get. Goodbye Stratos...it hasn't been pleasant.'

Stratos shrieked an inhuman chorus of agony. Random's face wore that of defiance and finality as he turned and sped away out of the hole.

As he pelted upwards, his speed and agility sending him flying up the shaft and using the momentum of the falling debris and buckled walkways, he could still hear Stratos' scream as he was pulled towards a fitting but very nasty death.

Stratos got to his feet gingerly and tried to follow after him but the damage to his circuits had spread to his legs and he crashed to the floor, his world burning all around where he lay.

Stratos tried all he could to free himself but the drag factor of the gravitational pull of the anomaly was starting to warp his metal body. Stratos watched as parts of him began to pull away and break. Little explosions where his circuitry was failing burst out all over him.

His optical sensors shut down.

He was blind but continued to hear the horrific screeching of chaos all around him.

He prayed for mercy that his bionic body would terminate itself, shut down to spare him the terrifying reality of what lay in store for him but it kept going right up until his final seconds.

It was happening again. His body was destroyed but he could still feel the icy grip of death engulf him once more.

Only this time, there was no way to cheat it.

*

Random dodged and weaved his way around the falling beams and fires that littered his journey back onto the bridge. He made his way over to the intercom and flicked a couple of switches, not really knowing what he was doing but hoping that he could make contact with anyone who could help him.

But he needn't have.

Within seconds, the same energy that had enveloped him on the Venus II shone its glowing light upon him again.

And as he faded away, Random smiled.

*

From the safety of her battle bridge, Admiral Bagari watched as the Orbital plunged deep into the anomaly. A colourful display of cosmic brilliance exploded across the view screen and a final blinding light and tremendous roar rippled across the entire battle fleet.

Some of her officers took cover as the amazing light bled all around them.

And yet within minutes, the light was gone.
The roar had faded to nothingness and the anomaly, the Orbital and Stratos were all gone…

Back on Earth, the gatherers on London Bridge whooped and cheered as they watched the incredible fire display. A burst of applause and hundreds of people whooping and cheering reverberated all around the world.

Dexter turned back to the newsflash he had got up on his work computer and stared in disbelief at what so-called experts were already surmising as a highly advanced light display.

He watched in astonishment as the newsreader said that there appeared to be no cause for alarm.

Instantly, he texted his wife, who had not seen his messages telling her that he loved her and that he was sorry for being forgetful all the time and reassured her that it was just a false alarm and that the world was not ending.

Yet.

Immediately, he picked up his office phone and punched some numbers into the keypad.

'Yes, get me the PM,' he said. He took his glasses off, rested them upon his desk top and rubbed his eyes. 'I know he's busy, but this is an emergency! I know everyone else is saying that but...look, I'm happy to hold, okay?'

The minutes drifted by until finally, the terminable hold music ended abruptly.

'Prime Minister? Did you just...well, yes I'm sure it was just a fireworks display, but don't you think it looked too...real to be...no, no I suppose you're right...yes, we do have much more important things to get on with than just ano...sorry, what do you mean by another alien invasion!?'

Meanwhile in Brooklyn, the little girl gave out a cry as she saw the weird spaceship looking thing in the sky disappear.

As soon as it went, she wondered if what she had just seen had indeed been real. Her Mum was always telling her what an overexcited imagination she had.

Sighing, she picked up her basketball and steadied herself.

This time she was definitely going to shoot through the hoop.

As she took her shot, the ball travelled through the air...and as the ball sailed through the net she suddenly had two reasons to smile today.

*

Random re-materialised in the familiar mess that was the Venus II's mid-section. He heard the smash of crockery under his foot and immediately realised that he had reappeared on top of Anji's favourite mug.

He'd beamed back on top of the table!

Anji, Jake and Skateboard appeared in the cockpit doorway and tore towards their friend. Random jumped down and gave them all a warm embrace..

'I'm so happy that you are safe!' said Anji, tears trickling down her cheeks. 'And I told you Skateboard...didn't I say all along that we could beam him up!'

'That you did, miss, it seems that we did it just in time!'

'How?' asked Random.

'Skateboard found the command code when he hacked the Orbital's mainframe. So with its shields down he could throw the transporter into reverse and give you a return trip.' replied Anji, squeezing Random tightly.

Random blew his cheeks out. 'For a while there I really thought that was a one-way ticket...'

'So Stratos is gone?' asked Jake. 'There's no way he can ever return?'

'You saw the Orbital plug up the anomaly...it's all gone now,' Skateboard reassured him.

Random's head fell.

'Io gave her life to stop him. She succeeded. So many have suffered thanks to what that man has done...'

The group huddled together again, collected in their grief and relief.

Stratos was gone.

13

REFLECTION

Some time had passed since the day in which the universe was saved and the time felt right for the peoples of the galaxies to mourn the loss of so many.

Stratos' words had echoed back through Random's head every day between then and now.

His mark was indeed stained across the whole cosmos.

Planets and entire solar systems that had grown and supported many unique species over millennia had been blown away in just a few seconds.

All those cultures, all those races. All those people, gone in an instant.

And so, after Admiral Bagari and Admiralty of the Space Seals had officially pardoned Random and his friends of any association with the intergalactic terrorist known as Stratos, they were decorated for their part in the victory, which had now been dubbed "The Battle of the Solar System."

Bagari herself was awarded the Premiership of the Space Seals Corp and under her leadership one of the first things she wanted to do was reward those who had saved so many.

Random, Anji, Jake and Skateboard had all humbly accepted the Medal of Honour, which they were awarded during a ceremony on the Space Seals HQ planet of Xarephas. But before the ceremony, Bagari had one request that she wanted them to fulfill.

That evening, the universe turned off the lights. At a coordinated time, everywhere went black. And then, little white lights began to fade into existence on Xarephas. The entire planet began to twinkle as its residents all lit a candle and held it in their hands.

Its neighbouring planet, Dorva, did exactly the same. Then its neighbours. Then the next planet along, and another.

Before long, every planet still in existence shone back into light as everyone held a candle high for those who had perished and for those planets that were no longer there.

For the stars that were no longer in the sky. Random and his friends looked up and around them as they and millions upon millions of others showed solidarity and remembrance.

When Bagari had asked them to take part, there was nothing else they felt they should do.

It was an honour for them all and a reminder to them that even in the darkest situation there can always be light…

As the travellers said their goodbyes, Random shook hands with Bagari, who had offered to see them off.

'Captain,' she said dryly.

'Admiral,' he said back.

'Once again, on behalf of the Space Seals Corp I thank you all for what you have done.'

'Ah,' Random snorted. 'All in a day's work for us.'

'I take it that if we need your co-operation again then you will give it?'

'Of course,' he smiled. 'You know where to find us.'

Bagari frowned. 'Actually, we don't.'

Random began to follow his friends up the platform into the Venus II.

'Ah, that's okay, if there is trouble, you can be sure it will find us first. Until next time, Bagari.'

'Let's hope there isn't one,' she said as the platform raised fully and the Venus II, cleared for take-off by the Space Seals air traffic control, rose high in the air and flew majestically back out into space and far away from Bagari and Xarephas.

A while later, the crew of the Venus II were gathered in the cockpit as Random stood behind Jake, who was occupying the pilot's seat, watching with bated breath.

'Okay, Skateboard, stabilisers off!'
Random and Anji held onto the nearest solid fixtures for dear life as Skateboard silently clamped himself magnetically to the floor. But the Venus II didn't jolt, didn't stutter to a halt or stall completely.

'I've done it!' exclaimed Jake. 'I can fly this thing! I mean, I knew I could but still, big moment for me, this.'

'Yes, Jake,' said Random looking at Anji in disbelief. 'Seems that you can.'

'My turn next!' cried Anji.

'About time too,' smiled Random.

'So, Bagari's going to become the leader of the Space Seals then?' said Jake.

'She deserves it,' Anji replied.

'Yeah, and so did we!' said Jake, taking his hand off the steering wheel to kiss the medal that he still had draped around his neck. The Venus II buffeted a bit as he did so.

'Eyes on the road, Jake!' said Anji.

'Sorry, you lot,' he said shame faced.

'I'll put it on auto-pilot,' said Skateboard.

'Cool, so where to next?' asked Random.

'Well, first of all maybe we should get you looked at again,' said Anji.

'Why?'

'Have you not noticed? You're still red and blue!'

Random took a look at his reflection in the view screen.

'Yeah...well, the rest of me seems fine again. Run a scan over me if you don't believe me, I feel like I'm back to my former self!'

'Yeah, but you don't look it!' said Jake.

'Maybe it's time I showed my true colours...' Random said to no one in particular. He looked up at his friends and grinned and made his way out into the mid-section.

'As for where we go next, I'm easy, but somewhere quiet would be good. After all we've been through. You'll never hear me grumbling about having to go on holiday again!' he said.

Anji laughed as she too made her way after him before Jake's hand pulled on her sleeve.

'Er...Anj, can I have a minute?'

The pair walked back to the living quarters and sat on Jake's bed.

'Listen, I don't want to panic you or anything but...some quite nasty stuff happened to me when I was on board the Orbital. I don't want to talk about it now, but I will, I have promised that to myself. When I am ready.'

Anji looked concerned at her friend and placed her hand on his.

'But when I can, I want you to be the person that I talk to. Is that okay?'

Anji gave Jake a kind smile and leaned over to kiss his cheek.

'Of course.'

Jake smiled back, but Anji could sense that he wasn't quite right. The bravado had slipped. She wasn't going to tease him. They'd all seen some nasty stuff over the last few weeks.

'You just say the word and I'll be there.'

Jake pulled her in and gave Anji the biggest hug he could. He began to well up.

'You always are.'

Back inside the cockpit, Random was sitting on the floor with Skateboard helping his AI robot carry out his tasks of routine maintenance all the while filling his friend in on what had happened on the Orbital.

'So this torture technique...it restored your powers?' asked Skateboard.

'Yes. Not sure how.'

'I think I can explain it,' he said whilst shocking some new wiring into place under the dashboard. 'Your synaptic reflexes were rejuvenated by the electrical impulses. So, all the time Stratos thought he was making you weaker, he was in fact making you stronger.'

'Wow. I need to talk to Jake...he put up with so much. And Io...' Random broke off. 'I know you'll say I couldn't have given anymore but I'll always feel guilty I couldn't save her. And the rage...the anger I had for that man, that machine. If that other Random was just like me then no wonder he let the Flux overtake him.'

'But you didn't. And for that you are nothing like your alternate self.'

Random sighed. 'Yeah, I suppose you're right.'

'I often am,' said Skateboard.

Random moved forward to install another new set of wiring. Clumsily, he spilled his hot chocolate, making Skateboard jump who in turn accidentally shocked Random with one of the cables. A bolt of energy cracked loudly like a whip.

The robot watched in horror as the red/blue coloured boy tumbled backwards.

'Sir! Are you okay?'

Random groaned and Skateboard's diodes sighed.

'Really Skateboard,' he said as he picked himself up, 'You're so jumpy!'

Skateboard recoiled in surprise.

'What's up?'

'Sir, I think you should take a look for yourself...'

Random got to his feet and checked his reflection in the dashboard. He check it again. His skin seemed to be shifting, changing.

Anji and Jake raced into the cockpit.
'What's going on?' asked Anji. 'We thought we heard lightning!'

Random turned to face them, his face beaming with the biggest grin he'd had in a long time.

'Guys,' he said, utterly delighted. 'I'm purple again!'

ACKNOWLEDGEMENTS

With thanks to the usual cast of characters. To my wife Sophie for approving the early drafts, to Nicola Currie, Tom Savill-Owen, Stephen D'Costa, Anna Brown and Hannah Haynes for their sage advice.

To Richard James, Dr Sandifer, Steve Hayward, Mark John, Sci-Fi Room, Mark Cockram and Iain Martin for promotion and all the help along the way.

To Anthony Moorin whose brilliant artwork brings the worlds of Captain Random to life.

To Haverhill and Linton Libraries for them wanting to help promote the series.

To VC Covers who sew the cover art together and deal with the final tweaks.

And lastly, to yourself for buying and reading this book. Please do leave a review wherever you bought it as it really helps us writers find more readers just like you!

The adventures of Captain Random will continue
in JOURNEYS IN THE RANDOMVERSE.

ALSO AVAILABLE

The Lurking
ISBN: 978-1999865955

Rob is a hopeless loser in the game of life. With work, his relationship with his long suffering girlfriend Claire, with everything in general. Tonight he will change for the better, make a fresh start by taking it to the next step and propose to her.

But fate has other intentions.

After an accident that leaves him stranded, Rob takes shelter in an abandoned aircraft hangar and soon discovers that he is not alone. There is something lurking in the darkness, taunting him, haunting his every movement.

Soon trapped in a living nightmare, Rob must learn the terrible truth of his tormentor and escape its clutches before it is too late...

Available from all good book shops.

Captain Random and the Rainbow Chasers
ISBN: 978-1999865962

The Zedron Flux is the most powerful energy source in the known cosmos. In the right hands, it has the power to end all suffering. In the wrong hands, it could bring an end to all things. After a narrow escape from an army of ancient gods, Random, Anji, Jake and Skateboard crash land on the beautiful planet of Spectronia, a paradise of colour and home to a peaceful race ruled by the elegant Solenia and her Valkyries. Upon recovering they ally themselves with a band of explorers led by Lon, who is hell bent on finding the Flux after it was taken from his grasp by a rival archaeologist. But nothing for the crew of the Venus II is ever simple. As the quest continues, danger is not far away and, as the Flux gets closer and closer, Random is left with a terrible choice that will have major consequences, not just for him and his friends, but for the entire universe...

Captain Random and the Eater of Souls
ISBN: 978-1999865931

Following their explosive battle with the Sandman, and struggling to come to terms with life out in space, the crew of the Venus II decide to throw themselves into a spot of retail therapy on the friendly planet of Genocia.

But almost as soon as they arrive, they realise that this new world is not all that it seems. Outside the splendour and vast wealth of the Grand Chamber lies a neglected wasteland where terror lurks within the poisonous gloom whilst deep within the bowels of the planet lies a terrible secret.

At the very heart of it all is the ruthless leader Consula, whose designs for supremacy mean ultimate devastation to all of those who oppose her. But the greed and corruption of the government is nothing compared to what lurks in the shadows for Random and his friends. Separated and fighting for their lives, Random, Anji, Jake and Skateboard must work quickly to save the lives of the prisoners stuck in the mines deep below the surface, where death is very close by...

What is the Soul Destroyer? What part does it play in Consula's diabolical plan? Will Anji ever see her friends again? One thing is for sure. The Eater of Souls is hungry...

Captain Random vs the Sandman
ISBN: 978-1999865924

Rodas. The scorned planet of Ursa-17. Ravaged by centuries of war between two factions, the villainous Sapphire Regime and the ruthless Crimson Empire. The reason behind the conflict of red and blue? The people of Rodas were unable to make the colour purple.

Until one day, when two rebels, one from either side, combine to create the ultimate warrior. A being who could put an end to the battle of ages and bring peace to the volatile planet of Rodas once and for all.

There is one tiny drawback. The warrior is a boy.

***** Fantastic book, enjoyed every part of it! Highly recommend it for Dr Who/Red Dwarf/Rick and Morty fans.

***** Hayden Gribble's writing is witty and clever with an essence of Douglas Adams in there too. Would thoroughly recommend for anyone with an adventurous spirit.

***** I really enjoyed it. I can well imagine Kids getting swept along with the interstellar, action packed adventure and chuckling along with all the funny scenarios and characters and wanting to know just what happens .

Available from all good book shops.

Child Out of Time: Growing Up With Doctor Who
in the Wilderness Years
ISBN: 978-1999865900

For 26 years, DOCTOR WHO was a British institution, capturing the imaginations of generations of children. But then, in 1989, it was cancelled. The Doctor and his on-screen adventures were no more. There was no longer a hero, a champion for the outcasts who struggled to fit in. It was as though he had walked into his TARDIS and set his controls for dematerialisation, never to return: a whole generation lost to the powers of Science Fiction's greatest creation. It was in this Doctor-less world that I grew up. This is the story of how one little boy would try to find the Doctor in any way, shape or form and the obstacles he faced in doing so. This is the story of growing up without Doctor Who in the Wilderness Years...and how I lived through it.

***** An engaging and enjoyable insight into a fan discovering Doctor Who during the wilderness years

***** A very passionate account of one fans discovery of the greatest science fiction of all time.

**** Perfect for fans of the Doctor in any of his or her forms.

Available from all good book shops.

The Man In The Corner
ISBN: 978-1500549862

A mysterious assassin wants out of his life as a cold and ruthless killer but must face one last assignment before he flicks the escape switch. As he closes in on the biggest criminal mind in the country, he is reminded of what he left behind and how getting closer to the light at the end of the tunnel might also reunite him with a person from his long and distant past. Who is the Big Chief? Why must he be brought down and will it be the end, not just for himself and his superior, but also to the only link to the life he has lost.

***** An exciting book! Whilst focusing on the dark story of an unnamed man, you find yourself sucked into a city of criminals. The chapters contain their own stories which really draw you in and make you want to read more. Great read! The only negative is that it was over too fast.

***** Brilliant read. Did not want to put the book down.

*** This book is a great little read about the path to redemption; not too long, in fact in some places I found myself wishing it might go on a little longer. It's got a sort of style all its own.

Available from all good book shops.

Hayden Gribble was born in Cambridge in June 1989. He has always loved writing and released his debut novel, The Man In The Corner, as an eBook in 2013 before it went paperback the following year.

Since then, Hayden has managed to top the Amazon best seller list on three occasions, although the Booker Prize still seems some way off.

The Stratos Conundrum is Hayden's eighth book and the fourth in the Captain Random saga.

Away from writing, Hayden loves reading, walking, sports, music, film and TV.

He has also been a regular member of the Diddly Dum Podcast, a show about Doctor Who, since February 2015 and curates his own James Bond podcast, Podcasters Royale. Both can be found on iTunes.

He lives with his wife and son in Suffolk.

You can find out more about Hayden and Captain Random at www.haydengribbleauthor.com

www.ingramcontent.com/pod-product-compliance
Lightning Source LLC
Chambersburg PA
CBHW072029220726
48293CB00016B/601